D0485244

Murder in the

A Detective Capella Crime Novel
by
Jackie Holiday

This stand-alone novel, *Murder in the E.R.* features Detective Tony Capella. The books can be read in any order, however, they are best experienced in sequence.

Novels featuring Detective Capella in order:

Murder in the E.R.

Daughter of the Don

Weaver of Fate

A journey of daring and courage:
Two Against the Sea

The Girl in the Corner Office

Table of Contents

Chapter 1
The coffee shop

There is to be found a beauty in youth. No more so is this true than in a young person with a firm foothold as they set out on the journey of life. Nancy Miller was imbued, gifted with such a beauty: smooth of skin, clear of eye, on the cusp of a life destined for greatness, or if not greatness, then for a life to be admired.

"Pretty dress, hate the shoes." Nancy Miller flipped through her fashion magazine and took another sip of coffee, just as she did every morning. Nancy loved working in Boston, not just anywhere in town, but in Boston's Financial District. She looked out the coffee shop window and watched as well dressed people walked up and down the sidewalk heading to work; people to whom million dollar deals are a matter-of-course. Looking out the window, one couldn't tell if they were in London, Paris or New York. Nancy had wanted to live in New York, but "Daddy" had wanted to keep her close. Nancy was an only child, and her father spoiled her rotten.

As she did every morning, she turned her attention to the women waiting in line for their coffee and croissants. She sat back and started her critique: *Fake leather belt, way too big... Blue shoes and brown socks? Really? Call the fashion police... Time for another hair-dye, lady. Your roots are showing.*

Out of the corner of her eye she caught sight of a large handbag and had just enough time to think "*Gucci*" before it knocked her cup of coffee to the floor. Nancy held her breath as the plume of coffee rose into the air; luckily splashing away from her and her chic clothing. She wore: Vuitton pumps, Versace skirt, and her favorite Armani flowered blouse.

"Oh, I am so sorry!" A woman with a scarf tied about her head and Jackie O sunglasses grabbed up a few napkins. As she dabbed ineffectually at the coffee she asked, "Did it get you?"

Nancy looked down at her shapely legs. "No, I'm okay."

Standing, the woman asked, "What are you drinking, hon'? Let me get you another."

"That's okay. I really…"

"I insist. That was totally my fault."

Nancy said, "Okay, just a regular. Cream and two sugars."

"Be right back."

Nancy shook her head and went back to her magazine. When she looked up again, the woman was at the stainless counter putting a lid on her coffee cup.

"Here you go sweetie. Sorry about that." She set the cup down on the table and walked out.

Nancy looked at the time on her phone, and slid the magazines into her own bag. As she did so, she glanced at the silver bracelet on her wrist, a gift from her mother, and smiled. Her mother had been a model, and had died when Nancy was fifteen. In college her friends had often told her that she should be a model as well. Nancy had spoken to her father about a career in modeling, but he wouldn't hear of it. He had said in no uncertain tones, "Models spend their lives traveling and I want you close."

And when her mother had been alive, how she had traveled! Summers in Marseille, winters in Milan, parties, races and the shopping! Nancy and her mother would no sooner walk into a store then one of the sales girls would disappear, and return moments later with the owner, who would kiss their hands and tell them how beautiful she and her mother were. They would leave with bags over their arms bulging full of complementary clothing, shoes, and jewelry… all in the hopes that Nancy's mom would wear them and be photographed in them. Nancy had been groomed for modeling from an early age. She'd taken classes in poise, dance, aerobics, French, Spanish, and German. She'd been dubbed "the next big thing" and had several marriage proposals while still in high school. When her mother died in a car accident with her publicist, her father had changed all that; it was all business, and Nancy had embraced it with open arms. Daddy gave her the means and the encouragement she needed. Nancy and her father had become inseparable since the loss of her mother.

Nancy walked down the sidewalk with a spring in her step. The sky was a cobalt blue; white puffy clouds scudded across the sky and were reflected in the windows of the buildings and skyscrapers, giving the illusion of an endless horizon. Birds flitted between the flowering cherry trees, set at intervals in the concrete; city birds that were so tame they would take food from an outstretched hand. Unlike other parts of the city, where people looked careworn, harassed and tired, the workers of the financial district moved with purpose and carried themselves like aristocrats. Black capped Chauffeurs opened doors for executives.   Window cleaners worked with fervor, hurriedly finishing their early morning rounds so they would not commit the heinous sin of being seen by the elite.

Nancy stopped by a van unloading trays and trays of fresh flowers, which would adorn the lobbies, offices and meeting rooms where billion dollar deals were struck. Nancy bent down, closed her eyes, and inhaled greedily the scent of roses. One of the women readying the flowers was struck by Nancy's beauty and her appreciation of the flowers. She smiled and said, "Lovely aren't they? They just came in from Oregon."

Nancy sighed, "They're delightful."

The woman pulled half a dozen red, white and yellow roses, tied them with a piece of green ribbon, and handed them to Nancy, who smiled, inclined her head, and said, "Thank you, they're beautiful."

"Yes, but mind the thorns."

Nancy held the flowers so that she could breathe in their perfume as she continued her walk to work. As a breeze caught her hair, Nancy smiled showing her perfect teeth. Men stopped and stared as she walked by.

Whitney and Brown was one of, if not the largest law firms in Boston. Its marble façade, polished floors and glass elevators all proclaimed success. It was also one of the few places where all of the men wore suits. As Nancy walked toward the glass doors, a young security guard in the foyer walked quickly over and opened it for her with a flourish. "Good morning, Miss Miller."

"Good morning, Paul. Thank you."

"You look very nice today."

"Thank you, Paul." she said as she smiled.

As Nancy walked past the security desk toward the first bank of elevators, the other security guards looked up and smiled. From behind her, Nancy heard two of the guards whispering, "Sorry man, I got there first. Maybe tomorrow morning you can open the door for her."

The elevator doors opened at the top floor where the crème de la crème had their offices. The floors were covered in a rich blue carpet; the walls were an off white, with wood paneled wainscoting. Oil portraits in gilt frames hung every few feet, interspersed occasionally by a mirror or seascape. The portraits were of the company's present executives. Unlike other companies, when executives left Whitney and Brown, their portraits were promptly replaced.

As Nancy walked down the hall to her office, men leaned back in their chairs and peeked out their doors to catch a glimpse. The "big boss" had his office at the end of the hall. The higher you were "up the ladder" at Whitney and Brown, the closer your office was to the big boss. Nancy's office was three quarters of the way down the hall.

Nancy placed her coffee cup and flowers on her modern, black glass topped desk. She walked over to a cabinet and pulled down a clear French vase.

Carrying the vase, she strolled down to the ladies room, opened the door, and was greeted by the scent of half a dozen perfumes. Nancy wrinkled her nose in disgust. Quickly replacing her expression with one of confidence and greeting, she smiled at the reflection of the girls in the mirror. Some were touching up their makeup, and some, red eyed from a night of partying, were hurriedly and clumsily applying theirs. "Good morning, Nancy," they said, almost as one, like students greeting their teacher. They all looked up to Nancy, were envious and often jealous of her; not only for her good looks, but for her poise, professionalism, and her position on the company ladder. Nancy returned their greeting with a smile, "Good morning." Looking at her own reflection, Nancy turned her head from side to side, and thought *"Perfect."* She turned on the tap and filled the vase with warm water.

When she got back to her office, she arranged the roses, and took a seat in her black leather chair.

Comfortably settled, most secretaries would kick off their shoes, reach into a drawer and pull out a pair of sneakers. Nancy felt that was "sacrilege". Instead, she turned on her computer and checked her email. "Okay, delete, delete, look at that later, delete…" Nancy opened an email to her boss marked urgent:

Daniel,

Don't forget to pick up some dog treats for Max.

Love you, Rick

Nancy put a reminder on her phone to pick up dog treats on her lunch break.

She pulled up the days schedule and moved it to the left side of her screen, then pulled up the months schedule and pulled it to the right. A lawyer's schedule could change at any time, and she wanted to make sure there were enough open slots, in case Mr. Whitcomb was called into a meeting or into court.

Nancy had once thought about being an attorney. As a teenager, after her mother's death, Nancy had spent a great deal of time with her father, and had learned a great deal about business. Nancy's father had naturally met with many types of attorneys; real estate, corporate, tax... While Nancy's father had been deep in conversations with one of his lawyers, she had spent considerable time with his secretary. Nancy had learned that the secretary was a real power behind the lawyer. While the lawyers, in the high power financial law firms got burned out and replaced, the top secretaries made just as much money or more, and had far more privileges. They weren't sued, or as sometimes happened, imprisoned like lawyers.

Nancy checked and rechecked the schedule. She had her own schedule as well. If all went according to plan, she should be head secretary in two years.

As secretary to a partner in the firm, Nancy knew all the men, and all the men wanted to know Nancy.

"Hey, Nance."

Nancy took another sip of coffee and looked up from her computer. "Hey Bill," she said without much enthusiasm.

Bill put one elbow on her desk and leaned forward. "How about lunch today?"

Nancy kept her eyes on her computer screen. She was used to guys asking her out. Most thought it was a challenge. Bill was persistent, old enough to be her father, and he was married; the tan line where his wedding ring should be was a dead give-away. Nancy thought, "*I'll have to buy a frame with a picture of a cute guy in it to put on my desk. Maybe that'll act as a shark repellant. Either that, or a large can of bug spray.*" Nancy wasn't big on the dating scene. She had a healthy appetite like any young woman, but, for Nancy, dating just for the sake of dating wasn't worth the price. Most of her relationships had been one sided. She had been doted on and followed around like a puppy, and the endless, repetitive, meaningless texts such as: "You're so beautiful. I can't wait to see you." or "All my buddies are totally jealous and wish you were their girlfriend." made her want to tear her hair out. *Are all men so shallow?* Nancy liked being efficient, and hated wasting time. The guys she had dated seem more like vampires, sucking away her time and thinking, just because she was beautiful, that all she wanted to do was party, which could not have been further from the truth. Nancy would wait until she found a "real man" and married Bill was not that man.

Nancy shook her head. "Not today, Bill. Busy, busy."

Bill didn't move. He asked, "Maybe tomorrow?"

Nancy thought, *"Gee, can't this guy take a hint? I could tell him what he can do with his lunch, I should tell him, but he does play golf with the CEO every weekend..."* She temporized and said, "Maybe another time."

Still Bill stood his ground.

"Oh!" she exclaimed; her look of barely veiled disgust turning to a grimace of pain. Nancy closed her eyes and touched the center of her chest with the tips of her trembling fingers.

Bill straightened up, his look of eager anticipation replaced by one of concern. "Nancy, are you all right? You look a little pale."

"I'm fine. Thanks." Nancy shook her head and pulled up a spreadsheet. She leaned inward, bringing her face close to the screen, and rubbed her eyes. "I'd better call the tech guys, this computer screen's all fuzzy." Nancy reached for the phone and pushed it off of her desk with a clatter. "Why is the phone on the floor?" Her head whirled. The carpet irritated her cheek. "Why am I on the floor?"

She could hear Bill's voice, but his words seemed to be coming from a great distance. She squeezed her eyes tight shut, frowned and thought, *"Go away, Bill. Just go away...*"

"Wow, she's got a killer body."

"Thank you, nurse. Let's concentrate on her vitals shall we?"

"Yes, doctor." Nancy's naked body lay upon a sheet covered operating table. EKG wires and tubes snaked from her body to medical machines. Her auburn hair glistened under the severe white surgical lamps. She looked more like some futuristic cybernetics experiment than a human being. "BP 110 over 60. Respiration weak. Pupils dilated."

"Start a saline drip, with 50 cc's..."

"Blood pressure falling."

"Myocardial infarction?"

"I don't believe so. EKG is clean, let's get an echocardiogram..."

The doctor pulled one of the surgical lamps closer to Nancy's body. A group of young, white-coated interns stood on the periphery, watching the "best of the best" in action. They watched and remained silent. Dr. Pritchett had once thrown an intern out for clearing her throat.

"Blood pressure critical."

"Stand by with the De-fib."

The ER crew worked like a well-oiled machine, while the interns watched. Some looked apprehensive, some eager. One young man fled the room, hands over his mouth.

"100 cc's adrenaline," said the Doctor.

A nurse brought her head close to the doctor's, and in a hushed voice said, "100 cc's? Standard dose is 25, Doctor."

The doctor grabbed her by the shoulders, and through clenched teeth said, "We're losing her. Give her 100 cc's now!"

The nurse nodded and said, "Yes, Doctor." and jabbed a syringe into a glass vile. She injected the adrenaline into the IV...

"Blood pressure rising… 70 over 30…"

The interns breathed a collective sigh of relief.

A technician, seated in front of a computer screen monitoring blood pressure, pulse, O2 and EKG turned from her screen. "I've got an irregular rhythm here…" beeeeeeeeeeeeeeeep "Pulmonary failure."

The doctor looked about the room. "Where's that D-Fib?"

"Here Doctor."

"Stand back."   The doctor squirted gel on the defibrillator paddles and rubbed them together. "Clear!"

Nancy jerked as 3000 volts of electricity coursed through her body. Her back arched and her torso rose from the table.

"Clear!"

"Time of death 11:30 a.m." Dr. Pritchett put the defibrillator paddles down and asked, "Do we have medical records on this one? Is she a donor?"

A nurse typed rapidly on her keyboard. "Yes doctor. OPTN records indicate Nancy Miller; age 24, blood type AB negative… and… yes, we have a donor…" The nurse looked skeptically at her screen and said, "Doctor, you won't believe this. We have a match, and he's here in this hospital waiting for a kidney. Mustafa Califf. *The average wait for a kidney is five years, and this patient's been here five minutes…*"

The doctor looked about the room. "Okay people, start the clock. Let's get Mr. Califf down here stat. I want these kidneys in a pan before the recipient's under anesthesia."

The doctor picked up a scalpel, looked down at Nancy's flawless skin, and made a long incision…

As the trauma team made its way out of the surgical suite, the "cleanup" crew started to arrive. The mortician gazed at Nancy's naked body laid out on the sheet, her blue eyes open, unseeing. *"Could be a model… if she weren't dead. Oh well, another one for the collection.*" He darted a look over his shoulder, took a peek out the door, and pulled out his phone. Now sure that he was alone, he started snapping pictures.

Chapter 2
Red umbrellas

Deirdre had been given directions for her first delivery at the messenger service, picked up her empty satchel, slung it about her shoulder, and grabbed her bike, which was leaning against the wall among several others. When the service needed something delivered fast, they'd call on Deirdre. She hoisted her bike on her shoulder, and walked through the open front doors. Setting the tires down to the pavement, she mounted her bike, and set off down the streets of Boston. It was a mile and a half to the pickup spot, which she covered in only a few minutes. The sender was waiting just inside the front doors, which made Deirdre's life a lot easier. It still astounded her that people would want something delivered "as fast as possible", yet would waste precious minutes making Deirdre sign in to the building, find their office, or sometimes their very cubical itself.

An Orthodox Jew, with ringlets falling down to his shoulders and beard halfway down his chest, passed Deirdre a padded envelope, which she tucked into her canvas satchel and clasped securely. She signed for the package and handed the man her small clipboard. As the man signed, he read Deirdre's name on the sheet and said, "Please be very careful... Di..."

"It's Deirdre, pronounced DEER-dra."

"I cut the stones myself, Deirdre. If anything were to happen to them, I would be most upset."

"Don't worry. I haven't lost a package yet."

She had no doubt that she probably had a half a million dollars worth of diamonds in the canvas pouch on her chest. She'd carried many types of packages; documents, a change of clothing, a forgotten pair of shoes for a modeling shoot, the occasional love letter... One time she had even delivered a breakup letter. She had wanted to return to the sender and punch him right in the mouth for making her deliver that one. The woman who received it had fallen to her knees, and sobbed and sobbed. *What kind of man does that to a woman?*

Deirdre hopped back on her bike and headed south.

Most cyclists are tall and long limbed. At 5' 5", Deirdre wasn't "most cyclists". She was slim, well proportioned, and had none of the "thunder thighs" that some people who ride bicycles are prone to. Her legs, which would best be described as shapely and toned, were clad in a pair of old red gym shorts with white piping. Over a black sports bra, she wore a comfortable old gray cotton tank top. Blonde curls peeked out from beneath her helmet.

Deirdre zipped along, passing cars and other cyclists. Some, from their overloaded backpacks, were on their way to college, while others were out for exercise. She exulted when she passed men on bikes dressed in fantastically colored spandex, who, in their dreams, were training for the Tour de France. Occasionally she glanced down at the speedometer mounted on her handlebars and read 25, 30 or 35 mph.

She had been pulled over more than once for speeding. On one such occasion, she had begged the policeman to give her a ticket, and had said at the time, "Please, please give me a ticket. I'll frame it and put it above my fireplace. When I get a fireplace."

The policemen had laughed and sent her on her way, without a ticket.

She rode over iron bridges with rivers flowing underneath, through neighborhood parks, and through back alleys with overflowing dumpsters. When the traffic was too heavy, she'd nip over onto the sidewalk for a short stretch and then scoot back out onto the street. When she passed a row of hedges, she reached out and let the leaves brush against her fingertips. Every so often Deirdre would put a hand to her satchel, to make sure that the half million dollars in diamonds was still there. On runs like this, carrying something valuable, she'd sometimes think how easy it would be to skip the drop off, and fly down to Rio de Janeiro. Deirdre wasn't a thief, that wasn't in her character, but that didn't mean she couldn't have fun imagining it.

She took a drink from her water bottle and looked down at her digital odometer. She'd gone five and a half miles and had another mile to go.

She rode over the Mass Pike and its accompanying smell of diesel fuel. As she neared Fenway Park, she glanced at a group of people sitting in front of a cafe at wrought iron tables with bright red umbrellas.

That was the last thing she remembered: bright red umbrellas.

Deirdre's eyes fluttered open and just as quickly closed. The light was painfully bright. She opened one eye ever so slightly and, through her lashes, tried to make sense of... well, everything.

The last thing she remembered was riding her bike down Brookline Ave, near Fenway Park. *It was in the morning... The first run of the day...* She wondered, *"Where's my bike?"* Her eyes came into focus slowly. A row of beds ran along a wall of white tile. Machines and monitors stood beside her bed. She followed a clear tube with her eyes to find that it ended with a needle in her arm. *"I'm in a hospital."*

The woman in the next bed was shaking, curled up in the fetal position, her hair dirty and wild. Deirdre's brain worked sluggishly. She thought, *"Heroin. People get the shakes when they're coming off heroin..."*

People were moving purposely to and fro. Deirdre caught a glimpse of a woman in scrubs. She thought, *"A nurse."* and tried to call out, "Nurse!" but all she managed was a weak choking sound. She reached slowly up to her face with her right hand and felt her mouth. A plastic breathing tube was down her throat. Horrified, she tried to sit up. The world exploded in pain. Her breath came in ragged gasps. *"Oh, God!"* Her eyes rolled back and she passed out.

Chapter 3
The Black Horse

Tony put his razor down on the sink and ran a hand over his jaw. His deep brown eyes looked back. *"Good enough,"* he thought. Natalie had once asked him, "What's the difference between a close shave and a really close shave?"

When Tony had asked, "What?"

She had replied, "About an hour."

Tony's reflection frowned back at him. Natalie was his ex-girlfriend; the last ex in a long line of exes. *"Oh, well. I knew that one wouldn't last. She was pretty though... Pretty, smart, funny... Too bad she couldn't stop talking about her ex-boyfriend."*

Tony checked out his triceps in the mirror, not out of vanity, it was because it still surprised him that his muscles were so defined, so "cut". He hadn't made a conscious decision to be in great shape, it was the activities he loved that had made the decision for him: martial arts, rock climbing when he had the time, and being somewhat hyperactive. To the amusement of his friends and co-workers, he would treat any set of handrails that were close enough together as parallel bars. He put a dab of leave-in conditioner in his palms and rubbed them together. *"Haircut in a bottle. I'll go to the barber tomorrow."* He'd been so busy the last few weeks that he hadn't had a chance. He'd been on TV! Mom had loved that. Tony slapped on aftershave, wrapped a towel around his washboard abs, and walked into his bedroom.

Laid out on the bed was a pair of jeans and a comfortable short sleeve white cotton shirt. His sister had said that, with his tan, he looked good in white. Tony put on his sneakers. He picked up his backup 9mm sub-compact pistol, holstered it, and strapped it to his ankle. He checked his wallet to make sure he had enough cash for the night, grabbed his keys, and headed out the door.

Tony hopped into his Jeep, pulled out a finish nail that was stuck in the visor, and inserted it into a hole in the dashboard. It was simple kill switch, but an effective one. It would be embarrassing to have your car stolen when you were a cop, but Tony was no longer just a cop. He was now a detective.

The Black Horse pub was almost as old as Boston itself and was filled, as usual, on a Friday night. A black horse pranced on the wooden sign beside the door, and "Dubh Capall" stood out in gold letters across the bars face. Irish flags hung from the centuries old beams. Tony stopped and looked at one of the pictures of Irish "football" hung just inside the foyer. This was no usual Friday night for Tony Capella. This was the first Friday night for *Lieutenant Detective* Tony Capella. He took a deep breath, exhaled forcefully and pushed open the door to the pub.

His buddies had gathered out of uniform at the Black Horse to give Tony his sendoff. One cop, red-faced from drink and the heat of the room, put one hand on Tony's shoulder. He smiled and looked at Tony's detective badge, which hung from a lanyard about Tony's neck.

"That's a shiny new badge you got there, Tony. Very pretty." He turned to the bartender and shouted, "A round of drinks for the pretty new badge!"

Tony thought, *"A round of drinks for the whole bar! That's gonna cost a weeks' salary!"*

The pub was packed. There wasn't an empty chair. Most people were standing shoulder to shoulder, or sitting on the edges of the tables. Tony looked around and thought, *"If this place weren't filled with cops, the fire department would shut it down for a safety violation... unless it was filled with firemen."*

As Tony looked around at the smiling, laughing faces, he felt a pang of regret. He could almost always put a face to the voice he heard over the police radio, even if it were only a few words. Now those days were over. As a detective, he was now one of "them". Tony had an Uncle who'd spent some years in the Navy. When he was discharged he'd gone through a major culture shock. All he ever talked about were the "good old days". Some of his high school friends did the same. Tony felt that there was nothing as boring or as lame.

Tony looked around the bar and sought out the faces of his new "crew". Tony smiled. Leaning against the bar was "Sully" or Detective Sullivan: Tony's new partner. At six foot two, 285 pounds Sully was an imposing figure; despite the years and miles spent on his feet in a blue, officer's uniform, and being twenty pounds overweight. With his buzz cut and strong chin, Sully seemed more like a professional wrestler than a police detective. Tony and Sully went way back. When Tony's father had been alive, Sully would drop by all the time and eat dinner with Tony's family. There was nothing stuffy about Sully. He was as old school as you could get. Tony could see him across the room, joking and laughing with a couple of the "old guys".

A pretty young barmaid rushed by with a tray of drinks over her head and flashed Tony a smile. Tony had dated a barmaid once, but all she ever talked about was the bar: "...*and this guy was so drunk... And then this guy hits this guy in the head with a bottle... And another guy tried to pick me up...*" And she always seemed to smell like booze and stale beer. Too much drama. Not cool.

Tony looked over and saw Murphy, who was showing a couple of rookies the same old card trick. Tony called over, "Hey Murph! You ever gonna learn a new trick?"

Murphy laughed and flicked a card across the room at Tony, who grabbed it out of the air. Tony smiled. "Hey, I like that trick. You should lead with that one."

Tony wasn't surprised to not see any of his brothers or his sister. They were all married and didn't do the bar thing.

He saw them pretty often anyway, usually at his mother's house.

As the "man of the hour" Tony felt he should be socializing. He put his feet in motion and made a circuit of the Black Horse, patting people on the shoulder and saying "Hey." and "What's up?"

When he neared the bar, a group of cops surrounded him; some he knew well, some he didn't. One pressed a beer into his hand and said, "Tell us how you did it again."

Six years on the Boston Police Department and he'd made Detective. If truth be told, his promotion was due more from the news media than anything he'd done. He'd already told the story for what felt like the thousandth time. "It wasn't that hard really." said Tony as he put the beer down on the bar so he could better talk with his hands. "You know those exhaust fans at Park Street Station?"

"Yeah, they're like ten feet tall."

"Yeah. The ones that circulate air for the subway. The Red Line runs right under there. Well there was this white van parked in front of 'em (what he really said was "pahked" in his thick Boston accent. Like many Bostonians, his accent became thicker with emotion). So I get out to write this guy a ticket or have him towed if he was totally blockin' the fans." Tony grabbed a stool and sat as he continued, "So I walk up with my ticket book out, and out of the back door of the van, these two guys are feedin' a garden hose down the exhaust of the freakin' Red Line. They were sweatin' like bastards before they even saw me. And when they did see me they jumped and looked guilty as hell. I didn't know what was making them so damned nervous, but I pulled my gun and told 'em to drop."

"Yeah, I heard you kicked one in the nuts before he'd drop." said one cop.

"True, but when back-up arrived we found six 55 gallon drums in the back. Three with ammonia and three with bleach, and a pool pump hooked up to the battery. They were gonna mustard gas the T."

"Cowardly bastards." said Sully as he joined the group. "I wish I could get five minutes alone with 'em."

Smith, one of the "old guys" said, "What would you do Sully? Fall on 'em?"

Sully guffawed. He replied, "Get stuffed Smith, I'll kick the crap outta' ya', then I'll have you doing paperwork till you get as fat as me."

Smith joked back, "Good luck! I'm already as fat as you!"

A young cop worked his way through the crowd to Tony and asked, "Hey Tony. How come you didn't get a medal? Don't they give medals to the guys who bring down terrorists?"

Tony shook his head. "Hey, I got promoted, that's good enough for me. The FBI guys get the medals."

Some "local" in a group of twenty-something's sitting at the bar turned and asked, "What's with ammonia and bleach? Were they gonna' clean the T?" He looked to his pals with a big smirk, "It could use it."

Tony turned around and looked at the smiling youth. He had a split in his eyebrow and a bent nose from being broken, probably several times. He was the kind of guy who thought of bar-fighting as a recreational sport; a regular "badass". At 26, Tony knew that he was only a year or two older than this guy, but to Tony, this was a kid. Tony also knew what it was like to be a "badass". When he was 15 he'd been a "badass", too. Stitches, suspensions from school, broken knuckles, yeah, real "badass" stuff. That was until he got his butt kicked by a skinny kid. Preston Williamson was his name. Tony had started it in an effort to impress his friends; big mistake. When it was done the kid didn't kick him when he was down. He helped Tony up and invited him to his karate school. Later on he wrote Tony a letter of recommendation for the Police Academy. Now he and Preston were both cops and good friends.

Mr. Badass didn't intimidate Tony. When you're a third degree black belt, street fighting becomes kind of a joke. Tony sighed and, like a teacher speaking to a fifth grader, said, "Bleach and ammonia make mustard gas, Einstein. The Germans used it in World War I. Burns your freakin' lungs out."

Mr. "badass" wasn't smiling anymore.

Drinks came on trays and slid along the bar. Jokes and insults, some hardly distinguishable from one-another, flew back and forth. Tony sat with his chin in his hand thinking. A hand on his shoulder brought him out of his reverie. Sully leaned in to be heard over the noise of the bar and said, "Hey kid, take a walk with me."

Tony nodded and followed Sully out the front door. The night air felt cool and fresh after the closeness of the bar. Some of the faces had gotten a little too red and the bar a little too hot.

As they walked down the sidewalk, Sully glanced at Tony and asked, "Nervous about tomorrow?"

Tony shook his head, "Nah, different clothes, different badge, more paperwork... I'm a fast learner and I got you to show me the ropes."

Sully smiled, "You get to learn from the best."

As they rounded a corner they came upon a group of teens; boyfriends and girlfriends out for the night, with their arms around each other's shoulders, or holding hands. Tony smiled as they passed. Sully caught Tony's smile and asked, "You got a girlfriend Tony?"

"Nope. You been talkin' to my mother again, Sull?"

Sully had in fact been talking to Tony's mother. "You'd better watch out, or you'll end up a confirmed bachelor. You gotta' find yourself a nice girl."

Tony kicked a piece of asphalt with his toe. "Yeah, that's the trick, finding a *nice* girl."

"Come on, there's plenty of fish in the sea."

Tony laughed and said, "Yeah, too bad most of 'em are

barracudas."

Sully nodded. "Yeah, I've had my share of those."

They walked around the block and ended up back at the Black Horse. The night air felt good and Tony didn't relish the thought of wading through packed bodies. As Sully reached for the door handle Tony asked, "Think I need to go back in? It is my party, but I kinda' don't feel like it."

Sully shook his head and said, "They won't even miss ya'. Don't sweat it. To tell ya' the truth, I'm just as glad to get home and see the wife."

Tony nodded.

"Look, Tony, about tomorrow…"

"Yeah?"

"Better get a good night's sleep." Sully put a hand on Tony's shoulder. "I know you've been around the block, but when you're working homicide, you never know what the morning will bring. My first day was a murder-suicide, young couple, nasty."

"I've seen dead people, Sull."

"I know, I know. But it's different when you're the one responsible for bringing their killer to justice. You look a lot closer at a corpse when you're a detective. You look closer at their wounds, at their lives, their family, and their relationships. It can be heavy, Tony, really heavy."

"I gotcha, Sull."

"I'm just saying that you don't want to get too close to a case. I've seen good men lose it, Tony, and I mean lose their minds." Sully pointed his finger like a gun and said, "Like they were shot between the eyes with an age-ray. Grey hair, wrinkles, dying early… Stress will do nasty things to ya'."

Tony gave Sully a light punch to the shoulder and said, "I'm cool, Sully. Don't sweat it. Catch ya' tomorrow, OK?"

"Night, partner."

Chapter 4
You're awake

Deirdre could see soft light through her eyelids, though she was too afraid to open them. She bit down gently, slowly, until she felt her teeth come together. *"No breathing tube. Thank God."* She opened her eyes. The lights in her room were dim. She looked next to her for the shaking girl, but hers was the only bed in the room. She felt more than half asleep and her legs hurt. When she looked down at them, she found them covered with a sheet. Her left knee was raised so that her calf was parallel with the floor. She ran her hand over her face. It was scabbed and swollen. *"How long have I been here?"* she wondered. *"And where is here? I'm in a hospital, but which one? What happened to me?"*

She looked to the right and saw a head of bright purple hair. Asleep in a chair was a young woman. The only person in the world who would sport bright purple hair was her roommate. "Courtney?" she asked, this time relieved that the word had come out.

Courtney woke with a snort. "Deirdre? Deirdre, thank God, thank God." She stood and took Deirdre's hand in hers. Her eyes welled with tears.

"What happened, Courtney?"

"You were in an accident, Dee. It's okay now. I'm here. How do you feel? "

"Pretty out of it, to tell the truth. How long have I been asleep?"

"Three days. The doctor wasn't sure if you'd ever wake up."

The door opened and the lights became painfully bright. "I see you're awake," said the doctor, as he took a flashlight from his pocket. "I'm Dr. Pritchett. How are you feeling, Deirdre?" he asked, as he shined the light in one eye, then the next, watching Deirdre's blue eyes dilate.

"You tell me, Doctor. I just got here."

"It's the head trauma we've been most concerned with. You've been in a coma for the past three days. We've postponed treatment of your other injuries until your body is strong enough to undergo surgery."

"*Three days?* Surgery?" Deirdre asked.

Dr. Pritchett walked over to the wall and flipped on the x-ray reading lamp. There were a lot of x-rays: arms, legs, pelvis, back, and head. "Your left tibia was essentially crushed in the accident. That's the larger of the two bones below the kneecap. It will require several operations and extensive rehabilitation, but I see no reason why you shouldn't regain complete function of your leg. You have two compressed discs in your spine, which should be addressed first, as they are putting pressure on your spinal cord, between the T4 and T5 vertebrae, as well as between the T7 and T8. That area of the spine is where most of your pain is coming from. The fracture to your skull, while dramatic, should heal on its own. No bone or splinters have entered the brain cavity. You were wearing a helmet I assume?"

Deirdre looked down in concentration. "I always wear a helmet, but I don't remember anything about the accident."

Doctor Pritchett nodded. He was tall, his back ramrod straight, just like his hair. He wore a heavily starched white shirt beneath his white coat, which was ironed and spotless. As he took Deirdre's pulse, she could see that his nails had been expertly manicured. He looked down his nose at Deirdre, and spoke in a dry monotone, as if he were discussing a lower form of life, rather than a patient. "That's not unusual. Patients often repress memories of situations of extreme pain or violence. It's an after effect of shock. You'll be going in for more x-rays and an MRI this afternoon, and surgery as soon as you're strong enough."

Deirdre looked up and asked, "Has anyone in my family been in to see me?"

Dr. Pritchett closed his clip-board case, "No, but I see that you've already had one visitor," Dr. Pritchett looked with distaste at Courtney's purple hair, "although visiting hours don't start for another hour."

Courtney put her hands on her hips and leaned forwards as she said, "Right, like I'm not gonna' see my besty."

Dr. Pritchett put his hands on his hips said gruffly, "In an hour, Miss. You may see your "besty" during regular visiting hours. She's *my* patient."

Courtney stood and looked up into the doctor's face. She matched his gruff tone as well as his bearing when she replied, "Yeah, well, she was *my* friend before she became *your* patient, *Doc*."

Monday morning found Tony and Sully at the Boston Trauma Center. Tony flashed his badge at the pretty young nurse behind the desk, "Can you tell me where I can find a Deirdre McDonough?"

The nurse smiled demurely and said, "She's in the I. C. U.; fourth floor of the Everett wing. Room 433."

"Thanks."

As they walked away, Sully punched Tony in the shoulder and said, "Hey I think she likes you. You should ask her out."

Tony, uncomfortable in his new suit, looked up at the ceiling as they walked down the hall. "You think I should ask every girl out."

"From what your mother tells me, you can't pass a pretty girl without getting her number. She told me how you brought one brunette home one day, and another the next day. She said you weren't very happy when she called the second girl the wrong name."

Tony chuckled and said, "It's funny now. Carol was ticked. Or was it Tammy? Anyway, I'm taking a break from the whole dating thing."

With a mock look of concern, Sully said, "You still like girls, Tony?" as he punched Tony again in the shoulder.

"Funny Sull, very funny. Yeah, I like girls. I just seem to attract the wrong ones. And I'm tired of the same old, same old."

"Come over the house this Wednesday night for dinner. My sister's coming, and she has a daughter. Nice kid. Works over at the corner market."

"Thanks, but I'm good, Sull."

"Just think about it."

The elevator doors slid open and they squeezed in with a family with flowers and a very pregnant woman.

They got off at the fourth floor, stopped at the nursing station, and walked to room 443. When Tony looked about the room, the first thing that grabbed his attention was an attractive blonde with bright blue eyes in a hospital bed. He stood for a moment, rooted to the spot, spellbound by the beauty of a girl who would have called herself plain. He thought, *"She's petite, thin... Any other girl I'd have thought too thin... Heavy, unruly, eyebrows more often seen in the Scottish… But they suit her."*

She looked up at him and her blue eyes met his brown. Tony's mouth dropped open. Sully cleared his throat, breaking the spell. He pulled his gaze away with a start, and took in the intravenous tubes, monitors, and the fact that lines and pulleys suspended her leg.

"Hello, Ms. McDonough. I'm Lieutenant Sullivan and this is my partner, Lieutenant Capella. We'd like to ask you a few questions."

Deirdre looked from Sully to Tony and stopped at Tony. *"He's handsome,"* she thought. *"A good build, too... 26, maybe 27 years old."*

Tony pulled out his phone, pulled up a "speech to text app" and tapped "record". Feeling somewhat at a loss in

Deirdre's presence, somewhat embarrassed and a little confused by his embarrassment, he used his most officious voice and said, "You look a great deal better than when we were here last, Miss McDonough."

Deirdre looked puzzled. "You were here before? I think I would have remembered you."

Tony, in a more natural tone, said, "Well, you were unconscious at the time."

Deirdre ran her fingers through her hair. *"I haven't touched my hair once since I came to the hospital! And I have no makeup on! Not even lip-gloss! Great, that's just great."* she thought.

Tony could see that Deirdre looked uncomfortable, though he didn't know why. "We could come back another time if you'd like."

"No. No, that's okay, but I really don't remember anything about the accident."

Tony pulled a chair up next to her bed and sat down. "Can you tell me what you do remember? You were in a hit and run accident and that's a felony in Massachusetts."

Deirdre pressed a button on her bed control, so that she was sitting up a bit more. She grimaced in pain, and took a quick intake of breath between her teeth. Pushing the pain aside, she said, "Well, I got up at 5:30 like I do every day, had some juice, stretched out, and rode my bike to work. I work at the Foley Bike Messenger Service. I've been there about a year and I've never had an accident. It was my first delivery of the day. I rode about five miles and I ended up here."

Tony held his phone between them as it recorded, "Did you see the car that hit you?"

Deirdre shook her head. "Like I said, I don't remember a thing. Hey, do you know where my bike is?"

Sully looked up from his notepad. "It's down at the station. The lab guys lifted some blue paint from the car that hit you. The word is out to all the body shops to look for a dark blue vehicle with passenger side damage. Oh, and the package you were delivering has been delivered."

Deirdre frowned, she was glad the diamonds were delivered, after all, she had signed for them. She looked to Tony and said, "I really like that bike."

Tony put his hand on her shoulder, "I'll make sure you get your bike back, don't worry."

Deirdre smiled. "I'd appreciate it. I love that bike."

Tony marveled at this girl in the hospital bed. She was all scraped up, with tubes sticking out of her arms... she'd just been hit by a car and she was worried about her bike! She was tough, strong, and feminine at the same time... Tony asked, "What kind of bike is it?"

"It's an old Motobecane. I picked it up at a yard sale for 50 bucks; put some new beefy tires on it, and a new seat. It doesn't look like much, but it's fast and shifts really smooth, perfect size... It's like it was just made for me."

Tony put his hands on the bed rail and leaned in closer. "I know what you mean. I've got an old Jeep Cherokee that I've had for a long time. My mechanic told me I should get something "newer", but I just keep patching the rust. It drives like a champ. I'd be bummed if anything happened to it."

Sully looked up at the ceiling as Tony and Deirdre talked passionately about new tires and smooth shifting. He walked over to the window, sat on the air conditioner, and waited for them to wrap it up.

Tony was saying, "Yeah, it's an older jeep but it has low mileage and I got it for a great price. The only thing I couldn't stand was the clutch, so I took it to the vocational school automotive shop where my nephew goes. When he went to change the clutch he found a leak in the five-speed transmission, so my nephew had said, "Hey, Uncle Tony, we have to pull your transmission, and to get at that we need to pull the exhaust. Want me to put in a new exhaust? I told him, "Yeah, do what you have to do." My nephew took me at my word, and not only did he put in a racing clutch, he put in a racing exhaust, cold air intake, higher gears in the rear end, and a racing chip. It's one hell of a fast jeep."

Deirdre smiled at his enthusiasm and said, "I changed all the gears on my bike. I think what really made a difference was the chain oil. You wouldn't believe how many different types and brands of chain oil there are. Some of them gunk up in the cold weather, and some of them are too thin and are gone before you know it. I found one that I really like a few weeks ago. And it smells so good too! I actually..." she blushed "It smells so good I put some in my hair."

"Shut up."

"No, really, I did."

"Synthetic or natural?"

"Natural of course. My roommate, she works in a salon, told me I was nuts..."

It was almost lunchtime. Sully cleared his throat and said, "Well, I think that wraps it up here." and started reaching into his jacket pocket.

Tony beat him to it and pulled out his card first, which read: **Lieut. Tony Capella Boston PD** Phone: 555-0179. He passed the card to Deirdre and said, "If you can think of anything at all, or remember anything about the accident, please give me a call... I mean us a call," he stammered, "I mean the Boston Police Department."

Deirdre took the card, smiled and said, "I'll do that."

Tony and Sully made their way back to the elevator. As they passed the nurses station, Sully asked, "Was I hearing things, or did you just have a conversation with a young woman about oil viscosity?"

Tony stopped, scratched the back of his neck and said, "Yeah. Weird, huh?" He shifted his weight from one foot to the other and said, Hey, Sull..."

Sully looked at his partner with barely concealed amusement and asked, "You forget something, Tony?" as he pointed with his chin back towards Deirdre's room.

The color rose in Tony's cheeks but he smiled and said, "Shut up, Sully. Just give me a minute, will you?"

Sully, hands on his hips, said, "I'll do ya one better. There's a sandwich shop across the street from the hospital that's pretty good. Meet me there in, say, half an hour?"

Tony thumped Sully on the arm, smiled and said, "Thanks partner."

As tony sped back to Deirdre's room, Sully said under his breath, "Go get 'er tiger."

Chapter 5
There are no rules

Tony bounced on the balls of his feet and eyed his opponent. Preston lunged in and threw a sidekick. Like always, Preston was fast. Tony blocked the sidekick, and instead of throwing a strike, lunged himself bodily into Preston. Preston gave a grunt as they both went down onto the mat. Instead of picking themselves up and brushing themselves off, Tony and Preston continued to fight, not in the style of mixed martial arts where they have "rules", this was karate, where there are no rules.

A group of students had gathered to watch as they usually did, open mouthed and eyes wide. Tony and Preston had been sparring partners for so many years that they were able to execute martial arts moves that were seldom seen in the ring, moves that were beyond dangerous, moves that were deadly. Back and forth they moved, strike and counterstrike. Switching martial arts styles at will, from kung fu to jujitsu to karate, and fast, unbelievably fast. The instructor gave up yelling at them years ago. For one thing it didn't do any good, and for another, it attracted new students.

Preston got Tony in a chokehold, the one place Tony didn't like to be. Preston was strong, real strong. Some of the guys called Preston, "John Henry" from the old story *John Henry was a Steel Drivin' Man*, but never to his face. He intimidated the hell out of most students.

Now Preston had a massive arm around Tony's neck and was squeezing… Tony turned his head to the side and slowly wriggled, pushed, and forced his fingers between his own throat and Preston's forearm. Then he pulled down with all his might and managed to get a breath. "You're done Tony, I got you."

"Yeah, take a look at my other hand."

Preston looked down and saw Tony's hand just above his own groin. "Damn, maybe we're both done."

At the end of the class sensei pulled out the weapons. Every class ended with a different unconventional martial arts exercise, and weapons was one of Tony's favorites. The theory was that the best swordsmen made the best fighters. Sometimes the instructor would assign weapons, but today the students were free to choose. Sensei would clap his hands and shout "weapons!" and students would collect wooden swords and bo-staffs for the intermediate students. The advanced students would use metal blades that sensei had run a file over, just to take off the edge: spears, hook swords, tai chi swords and kamas, to name a few.

Sensei spun two rubber knives to see who would go first. When the knives hit the ground and stopped, the two students they pointed to stepped into the center of the room with their weapons. Jane stepped in with her twin metal tai chi swords. At 17, she was one of the youngest students in the adult class. Jane was tall, graceful, and aggressive as all get out. She intimidated students even more than Preston when she had her two swords. Ben, a muscular 25-year-old stepped into the ring with a wooden katana. The instructor said, "Slow motion" and then, "Begin!" All students started weapons class in slow motion for two reasons: One, so the instructor could gauge the student's control, and Two: one can't cheat while fighting in slow motion. If stances were bad, the student would hear it: "Why are you on your tippy toes, you want to take ballet? Go take ballet." Sensei didn't mean it as a put-down. Several of the students were accomplished ballerinas as well as accomplished martial artists.

Ben moved with a strike to Jane's head, followed by one to the side. Jane blocked with her left sword, threw a front kick with her right foot and brought her other sword to Ben's ribs all in one graceful movement. Ben was "dead".

Sensei stopped the action.   He liked to challenge the students, so he pointed to Tony and signaled him to join Ben against Jane. Now it was two against one. Tony traded his katana for a long staff. He liked to keep his distance with Jane. As Ben moved to the left, Tony moved to the right with his staff. Tony extended his bo-staff towards Jane's eyes, hoping to distract her long enough for Ben to close with his katana, a forlorn hope. Jane deflected Tony's staff with a flick of her wrist, dropped into a low leaning stance, and brought her other sword to Tony's ankle. Tony raised his hands in defeat and stepped off the mat.

Watching Jane and Ben fight was a thing of beauty. In the martial arts there is hard and soft, mountain and river, yin and yang. Ben was a big dude, but he could kick high and move fast. Blocking one of his punches was like blocking a tree. You had to move out of the way when you blocked Ben, or you'd feel it in the morning. Jane and Ben circled each other and then came together quickly in a flurry of strikes, Ben's heavier katana sliding off the edge of one of Jane's flexible Tai chi swords. Ben's motions were strong and linear, while Jane's were fluid, circular, and graceful. Ben came in close and somehow managed to grab one of Jane's wrists. Jane planted both feet as Ben started pulling her in. As Ben went for a leg sweep, Jane gave him a roundhouse kick to the chest and brought the flat of her blade against Ben's back, ending the fight. Ben stepped off the mat.

The Instructor increased the odds against Jane and sent three students against her, then four.   Undefeated, Jane smiled at the class. Sensei stepped onto the mat with a look of disgust, one that none of the advanced students took seriously, waved them off the mat and told Jane to get a drink.

As the workout progressed, the instructor increased the speed until there were no limits. It was like watching a kung fu movie. The students fought singularly, in pairs, and sometimes five against five.

Tony found himself facing John. They were about the same age and build. John was a natural and was really fast. John's reactions were so quick that Tony had asked him one day how many of his family members were pilots, who are known to have fast reflexes. John had replied "civilian or military?" The instructor held two rubber knives by the handles and said, "Knife fighting. When the knives hit the ground, pick up your knife and begin."

He then made to toss both knives down on the mat in front of Tony and John. The only thing was… he only dropped one knife in front of John. This didn't surprise Tony; his instructor had a sense of humor.

Tony and John bowed. Tony got into a light half-moon stance, ready to lunge this way or that, depending on what John did. John was no rookie. He came in with a sidekick followed by a lunge with the knife. Tony came down with his right palm with the intention of doing jujitsu, but John pulled the knife back and went for a horizontal strike across the chest. Tony lunged backwards and quickly lunged forward as the blade swept by. Tony had John by the wrist and they exchanged some soft to medium strikes to the body. John lost his knife and it slid across the floor. Instead of going for the knife, tempting as it was, Tony pressed his advantage and drove John's face into the mat. The instructor called a halt, told John to pick up his knife, and then tossed him another. John grinned at Tony. Tony smiled back and said, "Don't get cocky." He then walked over and took a bo-staff out of one of the watching student's hands. John flipped the knife a half turn in the air, caught it by the blade, and raised it to his temple as if he were going to throw the knife at Tony. Tony laughed; they both knew it was illegal to throw knives, even rubber knives, in class. The instructor laughed as well, called everyone to line up, and dismissed the class.

Tony and Preston sat down on a bench made out of a couple of milk crates and a 2 x 6. The studio wasn't really what you'd expect. It was more like a warehouse rented out by their karate instructor. The windows hadn't been cleaned in twenty years, and half the lights didn't work, but that didn't matter. Karate mattered. Some martial artists studied Zen, some studied chi. Here you fought. Tony remembered the time a student asked sensei, "What frame of mind should I be in when I am fighting?"

His instructor had replied, "Frame of mind? Just fight, and you're fighting will put you in the right frame of mind."

Preston wiped the sweat from his brow and asked, "So what's up, Tony? How was your first day at being a detective?"

"All right, all right. I met a girl. "

Preston smiled, "A girl, huh? First day and you meet a girl? You move fast."

"Yeah, you're one to talk. You got married at 17, right?"

"Yeah, but I'm still married, and happily. That's more than most guys can say."

"I'm not dissin' ya'."

"Yeah, I know. So tell me about this girl."

Tony stretched his back and said, "Her names Deirdre."

"An Irish girl, huh. Your mothers gonna love that."

Tony rolled his eyes. "I just met her today in the hospital. She got hit by a car."

"Damn Tony. Whatchu want a girl that's been hit by a car for? How about a nice girl that ain't been hit by a car?"

"Funny, Preston, really funny. You're like a freakin' comedian. No, this girl's nice. I mean, I think she's nice. I only talked to her for a little while, but there was something there. I don't know. It's like we connected somehow. She looked pretty, I mean, even in a hospital bed. That's got to be hard to do. I mean, imagine what she would look like normally?"

"You mean before she got hit by the car?" Preston laughed and punched Tony in the shoulder. "I'm glad you met a girl though."

Chapter 6
Spaghetti sauce

On Saturday Tony took a shower, changed, and headed over to his mother's house for dinner. He liked to stop by at least once a week.

When he got to his mother's he sprang up the concrete steps, opened the front door, and headed straight for the kitchen, where his mother was usually to be found reading a book or chatting on the phone. When he got to the kitchen she was chatting all right, and sitting opposite her at the kitchen table was Sully, with a big plate of spaghetti in front of him.

Tony laughed. "Didn't I see you at work today? What, can't get enough of me?"

Sully chuckled and said, "Hey, your mom made me promise to tell her how your first day as a detective went. I think she figured a little spaghetti would help loosen my tongue." Sully turned to Tony's mother and said, "Sophie, you gotta tell my wife how you make your spaghetti sauce."

Tony's mother shook her head and said, "Sully, I've told Brenda, I don't know how many times, how to make the sauce. She still not doing it right?"

Sully rolled his eyes. "Not by a long shot."

Tony walked over to a cabinet, took out a bowl, went to the stove and filled it with spaghetti. "Mom, you do make the best spaghetti sauce in the world. Remember when all my friends used to come over after school, just to have your spaghetti?"

"I remember. Some of them still come around."

Tony laughed at that, but the funny thing was, it was true. When Tony was a teenager, he'd been over a friend's house and had opened the refrigerator and exclaimed, "Hey, my mom has a bowl just like this!"

It was an antique, light green bowl with white hot air balloons running around it. His friend had replied, "Yeah, I stopped by your house and your mom sent me home with spaghetti."

Tony's mother had probably fed half the neighborhood.

She looked down at Sully and started ticking ingredients off on her fingers, "You need fresh zucchini, a nice big onion, the best is the Vidalia, three cans of tomato paste, two cans of whole tomatoes, or fresh if you can get 'em, a couple of bay leaves, you want to pull them out before you serve the sauce so no nobody chokes to death... "Sully pulled out his notepad and started writing frantically, "Basil, parsley, some oregano, all fresh if you can get it, a couple o' cloves of garlic, you want to crush them with the side of the chef's knife, and then slice them up really thin, so you can see that nice liquid. The first thing you want to do is take some ground pork, veal and beef, nice cuts, no gristle, toss it in a pan with the cut up onion and a little olive oil, and sauté it so it's nice and brown. Don't brown the garlic whatever you do, it'll get bitter, and ruin the whole sauce. Then you take the meat, the tomato paste, the whole tomatoes and two cans of water, put 'em in a pot, and get that going. Dump everything else in the pot, and add a tablespoon of honey... Did I say zucchini?"

Sully looked at his notepad, "Yep."

"How about red bell peppers?"

Sully jotted down red bell peppers.

"You want to cook everything down until you get a nice dark sauce."

Sully tapped his pencil on his notepad and asked, "How long do you cook it down for?"

Tony's mother said, "As long as it takes. It might be an hour, might be two hours."

Tony put down his fork and said, "Look Mom, I hate to eat and run, but I gotta go."

Her brows came together. "What, I get five minutes with you? Where are you off to that's so important?

Sometimes I think that's my name, "I gotta' go" I hear it all the time."

Tony looked sheepishly at Sully, then said to his mother, "Well... I met this girl today at the hospital..."

Sully interrupted and said, "The one that was hit by a car?"

Tony's mother stood up and gestured wildly with her hands, "Hit by a car! What do you want with a girl that's been hit by a car? How about a nice ordinary girl that hasn't been hit by a car?"

Tony let out a sigh. "There happens to be a shortage of nice girls out there Mom. Believe me. I think I can overlook a little car hittin' for someone who's nice, don'tcha think?"

Tony's mother put her hands over her head, looked at the ceiling and said, "God, help this son of mine. He needs it."

Tony picked up a piece of garlic bread, stood up and said, "See ya', Mom. Love ya'. See ya' tomorrow, Sully," and headed out the door for the hospital.

When the door had closed behind Tony, his mother turned to Sully and asked, "Tell me the truth. How is he doing?"

Sully put down his fork and said, "He's doing fine Sophie. I'm training him old-school."

Tony's mother started picking up plates from the table and bringing them over to the sink, "Old-school? Whatta ya' mean old-school?"

"I'm training Tony the way I was trained. It's a lot tougher, but in the end he'll be a better detective, and he'll be able to take care of himself."

Tony's mother nodded, "I like the sound of that."

Sully got up, picked up his plate, and walked over to stand next to Tony's mother, "It's tough, really tough. But I see too many of the young guys making mistakes that I don't want to see Tony make. Most of the young guys couldn't cut the old training program, my training program, but Tony's got discipline and self control. He thinks with his head, not with his heart, and that's a good thing. I wish I could get him to trade that 9 mm peashooter in for a real gun though."

Tony's mother said, "I bought that gun for Tony when he started at the Academy. It was a Christmas present. You should have seen his face when he opened it Christmas morning."

"I bet. I remember my first gun. I have it right here." Sully said, as he patted the holster under his arm. "Maybe it's time for a new Christmas present. Tony couldn't say no to you, Sophie."

"Are you kiddin'? I wanted him to be a teacher or a carpenter. After what happened to his father... but now all my kids are cops. I never told any of 'em no. Sometimes I wonder if I should have, but then they'd probably resent me, and what mother wants that?"

Sully replied, "I could see Tony as a teacher. To tell you the truth, I was surprised when he joined the Academy."

"I was too. I could see all of my kids in law enforcement when they were little, but not Tony. Tony was always the dreamer; always off on some adventure." Sophie dried another plate and continued, "But he *is* in law enforcement now, just like his father..."

Sully put an arm around her shoulders. "Don't worry Sophie. I'm gonna look out for him."

Chapter 7
Hung up on rules

Deirdre put down her book and picked up another. She'd already read them all several times, but they were all old friends. She couldn't seem to get tired of reading about characters she had grown to love, and those she loved to hate. She was glad Courtney had brought them. Hospital magazines weren't the best reading material. Deirdre thought, "*Being in the hospital isn't only painful, it's boring.*" She missed her cat, she missed her bike riding, and she missed working in the city.

She'd moved to the city only a year ago, and she loved it. After four years of college, she'd tried working in an office, but found it suffocating. Sitting in a cubicle was as close to hell as she wanted to get. Her friends didn't understand. Her coworkers didn't understand. Her parents didn't understand. And so, after she'd given it more time than she should have, she quit her job, moved out, and took a job as a bike messenger in the city. Deirdre didn't mind the weather; sun, rain, snow, as long as she was outside and had the wind in her face she felt great, she felt alive.

She picked up the edge of her sheet and looked at herself. A week ago her legs were her pride and joy, toned, cut and muscular. Now one was swollen and gross, the other flabby, and both needed a shave. "I look like a Wookie."

"I wouldn't go that far."

Deirdre looked over her shoulder, "Courtney, where have you been? I've been going nuts here."

Courtney dumped two loaded shopping bags down on the chair, "Your mom called and said she had some things for you. I swung by and picked them up."

"Did she send anything good?"

"Let's find out." Courtney took the nearest bag and

upended it on the bed at Deirdre's side. "Okay, we've got your pajamas, from when you were like ten, towels, like they don't have these in the hospital, and here we go, a large box of tampons."

Deirdre sneered, "Gee, that gets me all warm and fuzzy. Thanks, mom."

"Don't worry, Dee, I've got you covered." Courtney picked up the other shopping bag, "Here we go. Everything a girl needs: face wash, moisturizer, shower gel, body lotion, tweezers, hair brush, toothbrush and toothpaste, razor and shaving gel, shampoo and conditioner, and last but not least, deodorant."

Deirdre sat up on her bed, "I would SO love to shave my legs right now, but I'm not supposed to. There's sort of a metal rod going through my leg."

Courtney picked up the shave gel and gave it a shake, "Dee, you get way too hung up on rules."

Courtney pulled up the sheet, started rubbing on the shave gel and said, "Gee, we could have done a bikini wax too. I wish I had thought of it."

Deirdre laughed, "Yeah, like that's ever going to happen."

Courtney shaved Deirdre's legs, rinsing the razor in the plastic hospital water carafe. Just as Courtney finished rubbing Deirdre's legs with moisturizer, Deirdre saw Courtney's eyes grow wide. And who should walk in but Detective Tony Capella.

"Hi, I heard this was a big day and thought I'd…" Tony looked down at Deirdre's freshly shaved legs, which he did not find flabby. No, not flabby at all. "I'm sorry. I should have knocked. I, I should really… I should probably go."

Courtney hopped up off the side of the bed, "No, I was just leaving. You should stay." Courtney pushed Tony into a chair. "I'll see you tomorrow, Dee. Love ya'."

As Courtney leaned down to give Deirdre a kiss on the forehead, Deirdre whispered, "Thank you, Court. You're the best."

"Yeah, well I um… I just wanted to stop by and see how you were doing."

Deirdre struggled between smiling and looking nonchalant, "That's cool. Did you find out who ran me over? "

"Not yet." Tony put his elbows on his knees and leaned forward, "We're working on it."

Deirdre propped herself up on one elbow, "No suit today?"

Tony was wearing jeans, Converse sneakers and a gray T-shirt. "Nah, today's my day off. I'm glad to be out of that suit. It's brand new and not very comfortable. I probably should have gotten one size bigger."

Deirdre smiled and blushed, "I thought it looked good."

Tony smiled and looked down at his shoes, "Thanks, yeah well… So did they say how long you'll be in the hospital?"

"They said that since I'm young and in good shape it ought to be 6 to 8 weeks, and then another few weeks for physical therapy. I don't know how I can do 6 to 8 weeks. I've only been here a few days, well conscious for a few days anyway, and I'm already going spazzy."

"Yeah, I hear ya'. My brother's a prison guard, and most of the guys doing time are in there for 6 to 8 years."

Deirdre's jaw dropped, "I'd escape!"

Tony laughed, "I bet you would. I could see you now, jumping over the fence."

"So are all of your family cops?"

"Pretty much. Two brothers, and my sister's a dispatcher for the state police."

"I thought about being a cop. I see the bike cops all the time when I'm making deliveries. I raced two of them once down along the Charles River. I kicked their butts!"

"I bet you did. Pretty competitive aren't cha?"

Deirdre smiled, "I've got brothers and sisters, too."

"They live around here?"

"Quincy. We don't talk much now though. We don't have much in common anymore. My mother's a control freak, and my brothers spend all their time in bars, or talking about bars. My little brother's the worst. He wants to be like his older brothers…"

As Deirdre talked, Tony took her in. *She has nice eyes. She looks into you, not at you.* He'd heard what Deirdre was saying before, from friends and on the job. Dysfunctional families are a dime a dozen. *That's probably why I don't have many friends. She has nice hair,* he thought *and nice eyebrows. I don't think I've ever thought about a girl having nice eyebrows before.*

Tony said, "Yeah, I see enough of that at work, before I became a detective anyway: domestics, bar fights, drunk driving accidents. If it wasn't for booze and drugs, I'd probably be out of a job."

"You make being a cop sound really attractive."

"No, it's not so bad. The hours stink, but I get to move around a lot," Tony smiled and said, "and I get to meet new people."

Deirdre blushed and looked down.

Tony stood as a doctor and several interns entered the room. Deirdre thought, *"This Doctor looks a lot nicer than the last one, that Dr. Pritchett."*

"Hello, Miss McDonough. I'm Dr. Clark. I'll be working on your back today." Dr. Clark looked like an old country doctor. He had rosy cheeks, a ready smile, and a twinkle in his eye. His bowtie would have looked out of place on most men, but looked right at home on Dr. Clark. Tony thought he looked somewhat like a Charles Dickens character. All that was missing was a gold pocket watch on a chain.

The doctor took Tony's hand and shook it "Is this Mr. McDonough?"

Tony blushed, "No, um, I was just visiting. I'll leave you to it. Do a good job, Doc." Tony put his hands on the side-rail of the bed, "Well, it was nice to see you Deirdre. Can I see you when you get out? I mean, after your operation?"

Deirdre's heart beat a little faster, "Okay, sure, I'd like that."

Tony had an urge to give her a kiss right then and there. He blushed, and gave her hand a squeeze instead, "Okay, I'll see you later, Deirdre. I'd better get to the station, I'm late as it is."

Tony gave the Doctor another look as if to say, *"You'd better do a good job."*

After Tony left, Dr. Clark held up a plastic model of a spine, "The disc is the cushion between vertebrae. When the outer part of the disc degenerates, or is damaged, the inner part can rupture or bulge. This bulging is called a herniated disc. Optimally we would have liked to perform an endoscopic microdiscectomy, however, your MRI shows a considerable herniation. Since you're young, and in excellent physical condition, I feel that an open discectomy is our best option. Under general anesthesia, a small incision is made over the center of your back. Once the herniating content that presses the nerve, or spine, is removed, the pressure will be relieved from the nerve, and the incision will be closed. This procedure is considered the most effective, and will benefit you most in the long term."

Deirdre took the model of the spine from Dr. Clark, although he seemed somewhat reluctant to let it go. "How long will it take to recover from the operation Doctor?"

"You'll have an immediate cessation of pain, and should regain normal movement and function within days, and by normal movement and function, we must take into consideration your other injuries. Dr. Pritchett will be able to give you a better idea of the timeline concerning those injuries. Do you have any questions or concerns?"

Deirdre shook her head, "Let's just get this over with Doctor."

Dr. Clark smiled and said, "Alright, Miss McDonough, let's get you prepped for surgery."

Once again, Deirdre's wrist band was checked, and she was asked to, "Sign here." She recalled first time a clipboard was proffered in front of her and she was asked to sign "for insurance purposes". She knew that she *had* insurance, but she'd always been so healthy, she'd never had to put it to the test. As she had signed the first "If insurance won't pay, I will" form, she had sighed and thought *"Oh, well. You can't get blood from a stone."* But a phone call to the insurance company had relieved her of her fear that her meager bank account would be bled dry with medical bills.

The nurse asked, "Any new allergies?"

Deirdre rolled her eyes and replied, "Not since the last time a nurse asked me that; which was, like, three hours ago."

"It's just standard procedure."

Deirdre sighed and said, "Sorry. I know you're just doing your job. I'm just anxious."

A young man, the anesthesiologist, entered the room and introduced himself, "Hello, Miss McDonough. I'm Dr. Thorpe. I'll be getting you ready for Dr. Clark. Have you ever had any trouble with anesthesia? Any adverse reactions?"

Deirdre shrugged and said, "I don't think so. The first time I've been under was here, in the E.R., just after my accident."

A nurse set a stainless tray with syringes and small vials of fluid on the side of Deirdre's bed. The doctor placed a green-tinted mask over her face and said, "Try to breathe evenly."

He checked the plastic IV catheter secured to her left arm before picking up a syringe. Deirdre's eyelids were getting heavy. She blinked rapidly as the gas started taking effect. Her voice muffled by the mask and her words slightly slurred, she said, "I feel pins and needles in my face."

The doctor was slipping in and out of focus. She heard him say, "That's perfectly normal."

The beating of her heart monitor seemed to grow louder, and the voices of the people around her softer, as she started slipping into unconsciousness.

Deirdre, eyes closed and completely relaxed, focused on the steady beeping of the heart monitor.

She heard Dr. Clark say, "Lets turn her over and get to work, shall we?"

"Yes, doctor."

Dr. Clark, the upper part of his face covered by magnifying surgical loupes, made a one-inch incision in Deirdre's back between the T4 and T5 vertebrae. The skin between her shoulder blades, colored yellow with antiseptic, parted under the scalpel. The doctor held out a gloved hand and said, "Retractors."

"Yes, Doctor."

Dr. Clark eased the retractors into the incision, under the subcutaneous tissue. He brought the handles together, opening the incision, and giving him a view of the operating site. Back bent, with practiced hands, he set to work removing muscle tissue from the bone above and below the affected disc. Deirdre, fully sedated, lay still, unaware, as the Doctor worked. Slowly, methodically, he gouged and cut the tissues. When, at last, he had a clear view, he removed the section of the disc protruding from the disc wall, and several small disc fragments that had been expelled from the disc. Pleased with his work, he closed the wound and started on the next discectomy between the T7 and T8 vertebrae.

Doctor Thorpe, the anesthesiologist, monitored Deirdre's vital signs. As was to be expected during a lengthy procedure, Deirdre's blood pressure was rising, as was her pulse and respiration. Her anesthesia was wearing off. Dr. Thorpe took a small bottle of clear liquid from the stainless tray and inserted a syringe. As he drew the fluid out of the bottle he frowned, looked at the label and asked, "What is this?"

The nurse leaned in closely to see the label for herself and said, "It's what you prescribed doctor."

Dr. Thorpe, still frowning, said, "It's not the usual bottle."

"No, Doctor, it isn't, but several companies have changed their packaging as of late."

Dr. Thorpe hesitated, but only for a moment before injecting the solution into the Y-needle injection site of the IV tube.

Dr. Thorpe suppressed a yawn and watched his monitor as Deirdre's blood pressure dropped to an acceptable level... And dropped further still.

An alarm sounded.

Dr. Clark looked up from his work, his hands poised over Deirdre's back, his instruments still.

Dr. Thorpe put his fingertips to the screen under Deirdre's EKG. Brows knitted, he studied the pattern and said, "Damn! She has an irregular rhythm."

With trembling hands, he reached quickly for another vile on the tray. He reached too quickly, the sleeve of his lab-coat catching the corner of the tray and sending it flying. Vials hit the floor and rolled in all directions: under the operating table, between nurse's feet...

The EKG flat-lined.

Dr, Thorpe cursed, "God damn it!" as he, and the nurses, scrambled on hands and knees searching for the one vial he wanted.

Dr. Clark was older, wiser and had more experience in dealing with emergencies than his young counterpart. He looked across Deirdre's body and said, "Nurse, help me flip her onto her back."

With deft hands, the two put Deirdre on her back. Dr. Clark, gloves still bloody, started CPR on Deirdre's lifeless body and said, "Call a Code Blue."

The code team arrived within moments with a crash cart and started work on resuscitating Deirdre. On the code team's arrival, Dr. Thorpe beat a hasty retreat through the still swinging doors, while Dr. Clark, still administering CPR, barked instructions at the code team.

Chapter 8
B. P. D.

Tony ran his fingertips across the new nameplate on his desk. It was made out of cheap, black, plastic with white lettering, but he was inordinately proud of it. Sully's desk was directly across from his, and front and center sat Sully's nameplate. It was large block of wood with **Lieutenant Sullivan** roughly painted in bright red letters. Sully saw Tony looking at it and said defensively, "My nephew made it when he was eight."

Tony had similar artistic renderings in his apartment. They were mainly finger paintings which covered most of his refrigerator, gifts from his nieces and nephews. "Nice job. Your nephew does good work."

Sully took a picture from his desk and spun it around, "This is my nephew."

Tony got up, walked over and sat on the corner of Sully's desk, and took the picture from Sully. It was of a group at the beach, and they were all on the hefty side. Tony pointed to the woman standing next to Sully's nephew, "Is this your sister?"

"Yeah, that's my sister Ginny. Hold on, I think I have a picture of her daughter." Sully rummaged through his desk, "Here we go. It was taken a year or so ago." Sully passed the picture to Tony. "What do you think? Pretty cute, huh?"

Tony took the picture. The girl looked surprisingly like Sully, only with long hair and bangs.

"Yeah, she's, um, pretty cute."

Sully leaned back in his chair, "You want me to set you two up?"

Tony put the picture down on the desk and said, "Thanks, Sully. But, I'm good. I appreciate it and everything but... Really, I'm good." Tony got up from

Sully's desk and walked back to his own, privately thankful for the escape he'd just made.

Tony sat down in front of his monitor and slid the mouse. He was figuring out the department's computer system on his own. Sully was supposed to train him, but Sully's computer, from long disuse, was covered with dust. Tony wanted to check if any of the body shops had reported a vehicle that could have been involved in Deirdre's hit and run. When he went to log in, the screen came up "PASSWORD REJECTED." "*I thought this was all set.*" he thought. "Hey Sully, I'm gonna to run downstairs to the I.T. department and see if they can straighten out my password."

Tony walked down the hall, stopped at the vending machine and grabbed a bag of cashews. He walked down the old metal edged steps that reminded him of his elementary school and made his way down to the tech guys. As he stepped into the office, a paper airplane flew by his face. One of the tech guys looked up guiltily. Tony cleared his throat, "Hey, I'm Tony Capella. Is this the I.T. department? Are you the guy to see about my password?"

A young, red headed, freckled man took his feet off his desk and said, "Yeah, I'm Sean. This is information technology. We, also, do all the electronics for forensics: hacking computers, video, and all the hidden surveillance stuff for you guys. Capella? I reset your password this morning."

Tony shrugged, "Well, it doesn't work now."

Sean scratched his head. "You do know that passwords are case sensitive, right?"

"Yeah, I do."

"Let me take a look." Sean tapped on his keyboard. "Sorry about that, I transposed two letters. It'll work now."

Sean stood up and walked over to Tony, "I was just takin' a break. You can only stare at a computer screen for so long before your eyes start whacking out." He scratched his neck and asked, "Ya' want the tour? I mean, you being the new guy…"

Sean looked eager to show off his tech-stuff so Tony said, "Sure, why not."

Sean led Tony out of his office, down the hall, and into the lab. It looked more like an Army Command and Control Center then what Tony thought a laboratory should look like. A horseshoe of video screens took up a good third of the room. Along one wall were benches covered with computers in various states of disassembly. Technicians hovered over keyboards and stared at video screens. None of them so much as looked up as Tony and Sean entered. They were all intent on their work.

"We do it all here," said Sean, "computer crimes, electronic evidence, video forensics, surveillance, enhancement… we do it all."

Tony looked around, "Impressive." Tony was impressed. His martial arts practice had made Tony appreciate the value of efficiency. If one could go directly from a block to a powerful strike, with minimum movement and energy, one had a great advantage over their opponent. If Tony were to sum up his first impression of the police electronics lab in one word, it would be "efficient". Tony was curious. "How did you get into electronic forensics?"

Sean ran a hand through his red hair, "When I was 13, I was one of the top hackers in the United States. I was only 13, so they didn't come down too hard on me when I got busted. My parents were cool. Instead of taking away my computer, they saw that it was something that I was good at, and they signed me up for computer classes at the community college. I graduated magna cum laude and I didn't even hack my grades."

Tony's eyebrows rose. He asked, "You were a hacker and you're working for the police department?"

"I'm on a, sort of, permanent probation. I know they're keeping an eye on me, but that's cool. I like what I do here and I'm not about to jeopardize it. I won't even pirate a movie off the net. They wanted me in the cyber crime unit originally, but I guess they didn't want to tempt me."

Tony looked around the lab and said, "I can imagine what a cyber criminal could do with this equipment."

Sean chuckled, "This stuff is antique to what they're using. The big guys anyway. They have a bigger budget than we do."

Sean walked Tony out of the lab and back to the I.T. office door. Tony shook his hand and said, "Hey, thanks for the tour. I'd better hit it. Oh, by the way, you wouldn't have a manual on the department's computer system would you? I could really use a roadmap."

Sean smiled and said, "There's no official "manual", but I can put something together for ya' pretty quick. I'll email it to ya'."

Tony said, "That sounds great."

Tony hadn't mentioned it to Sully, but the only thing about being a detective that Tony was apprehensive about was the computers. He'd had one in the squad car and used one to write up reports, but computers weren't really his thing.

When Tony got back to his desk, he sat down and found an old white coffee mug with BPD in big blue letters and *To Protect and to Serve* written underneath. Sully cleared his throat, "Your dad left that at my house a long time ago, kid. They don't make 'em like that anymore. It's been sitting on my shelf for years. I've never used it, and I thought you'd like it."

Tony stood and picked up the mug. He ran his thumb along the handle, "Thanks, Sully. I appreciate it."

"Your father would have been really proud of you, Tony." Sully motioned to the far side of the room, by the windows, "Your dad used to sit right over there. He liked to sit near the window. He hated the fluorescent lights. He said they hurt his eyes. Did you know that florescent lights flash 60 times a second? It's true. My wood shop teacher told me that if a table saw is spinning at a certain speed, the florescent light acts like a strobe light, and it can look like the blade's not even moving. That kind of gave me a fear of power tools. Did you know that videogames can give people seizures? It's all the flashing lights messing with their brains. Now think about it. A florescent light flashes 60 times a second, so people are sitting in offices, under these florescent lights, getting flashed 60 times a second..."

As Sully rattled on about fluorescent lights, Tony thought about his father. Tony was a teenager when his father had been killed. He never thought in terms of how many years ago it was, only the fact that he had been a teenager. His dad had been a detective, but he'd pick up a traffic detail whenever he could earn some extra money. He wanted to take the whole family to one of the theme parks in Orlando. The other kids in the neighborhood would come back from their vacations and talk about all the rides and all the fun they had, so instead of complaining, Tony's Dad worked around the clock whenever he could. It was on one of those details that he was killed. He was working on the Mass Pike, directing traffic around a construction crew one night, when a drunk driver doing 70 drove straight through the worksite. They'd said that he'd died instantly. Thankfully, Tony only thought about his father's death once in a blue moon. He preferred to remember him as he was.

He had a special place for his memories of his dad; they were like treasures that he kept in special treasure chests, to open once in a while and to saver. One of his favorites was when the whole family went to Nantasket Beach in Hull. They had all packed into the family station wagon. Tony had sat in the "way back" as he and his siblings had called it. The way back seat faced backwards so that he, one of his brothers and his sister would face out the back window. They'd make faces at the people driving behind them to see if they would make faces back. Sometimes the people would get mad, and sometimes they'd stretch their mouths with their pinkie fingers, or make a piggy nose. Once in a while an 18-wheeler would blow the air horn. Tony's father would smile and say, "Knock it off, you monkeys!" after he'd seen someone in his rear view mirror making a grotesque face.

Nantasket was always packed. When they hit the sand, Tony's older brothers would puff up their chests for all the girls in bikinis, and Tony would take his sister by the hand, to see that she didn't wander off. They'd haul all their gear: folding chairs, coolers, towels, and umbrellas halfway to the water's edge. If the waves were big enough, Tony's father would go down to body surf. He'd face the beach and do a "superman dive" just as the wave reached him. He'd float, seemingly effortlessly, on top of the wave. All the cool teenagers would body surf, but dad would put them to shame. When it was Tony's turn to learn to body surf his dad was very patient. Tony took twice as long as his brothers to "get it". When he finally did ride one into the beach, his dad picked him up, put him on his shoulders, and showed him off proudly.

Tony gave a deep sigh, and came back to reality, and to Sully's fluorescent light lecture. "That has to mess up your brain. I mean if someone said to you: Hey, let me flash this light in your eyes 60 times a second for eight hours a day, five days a week, you'd say "No". Anyone would say no. They'd say, no, that's freaky or you're crazy, get away from me! I'm not gonna' let you flash a light in my eyes 60 times a second. But, people do it every day. That's over a million flashes a day. No wonder so many people are messed up."

Tony rubbed his temples and said, "Thanks a lot Sully. Now I'm kind of freaked out. You sure know a lot of *stuff*. You know that?"

Sully put his hands behind his head and said, "I watch a lotta' TV."

The phone on Sully's desk rang and he answered, "Sullivan." His smile was wiped from his face. Tony knew something was wrong. Sully put the phone down and said, "That was the hospital. I asked them to keep us up to date on our hit-and-run victim. Tony, your new girlfriend, Deirdre, just went into cardiac arrest."

Chapter 9
I wanted to be a barber

Deirdre started to come back to herself slowly. Her pain wasn't nearly as sharp as it had been before the discectomy. It had been replaced by another type of pain, a soreness in her back and, surprisingly, in her chest. It felt as if she had taken a tumble skiing; a tumble all the way down the mountain. She struggled against the last of the anesthesia and tried to bring herself into the present. The ICU was dimly lit, but she could make out the vase of yellow flowers on the wheeled hospital bed table.

"Hey, how you doing?"

Deirdre turned her head to Tony, sitting in a hospital chair in the corner, and was surprised that the motion didn't hurt as it had before. With a weakened voice, she asked, "Tony? Hey."

Tony stood, crossed the room and said, "Thank God you're awake." He took Deirdre's hand. "You had a close call. I wasn't sure if-"

Tony's words were cut-off at the arrival of Dr. Clark and a trio of nurses. Dr. Clark said brusquely, "Clear the room, please." before ushering Tony out.

It was twenty minutes before a nurse came out and said, "The Doctor said that you can go in now, but only for a little while, and try not to excite her."

Tony asked, "Can you tell me what happened? I only got the bare-bones version form the nursing station."

"It was touch and go. I'd say she was lucky to be alive, but Dr. Clark worked like an animal to pull her through."

"Is she, I mean, how is she?"

"She'll be sore tomorrow but she should make a full recovery."

"But, what happened? I thought it was a straight forward

surgery."

"She had a reaction to the anesthesia. It happens sometimes; not often, and usually not so serious."

Tony tip-toed into the room, sat on the edge of a chair and said quietly, "I hope you like the flowers. I, um, never bought flowers before. The lady at the flower shop helped me pick them out."

"Thanks, and yes, I like flowers." She blushed.

Tony looked down at the floor, somewhat embarrassed. He could tell that Deirdre was still somewhat out of it. "Look, you just got out of surgery." He started to rise and said, "I can come back..."

Deirdre rubbed her eyes and mustered a smile. "No, I want you to stay. So, you never bought flowers before?"

"Well if you don't count proms." Tony sat back down and said, tentatively, "I went to like, six proms."

"Six?"

"Yeah, my senior prom was pretty bad. My date liked the limo driver more than she liked me. So when I was working at the pizza shop, there was this girl I worked with, and she was crying her eyes out. I asked her what was wrong and she said that she didn't have a date for the prom. She was like, seriously, 7 feet tall. So I took her to the prom. I didn't rent a tux or anything. I just wore an old blue suit, and drove my old Oldsmobile Cutlass. I vowed to be the best prom date ever since my prom was so bad. That prom picture was pretty funny. I came up to her shoulder, but I think she had a pretty good time. Then there was this girl with really bowed legs. She couldn't get a date for the prom either. I didn't mind the bowed legs, but then I went to pick her up. I knocked on her front door and could see trash piled up in front of her windows, on the *inside* of her house. And when I went inside there were cats everywhere, crawling over everything. There was a litter box on the kitchen table and a cat was doing his business."

Deirdre interrupted, "Please tell me you're making that

up.""

"Nope. I wish I were. When the girl came downstairs in her prom dress, I put the corsage on her wrist, and her mom took our picture in front of a pile of trash with cats all over it. That was pretty nasty. I'm pretty sure that was the last prom I went to."

Deirdre closed her eyes and shook her head, "Now you know why she couldn't get a date for the prom."

"Yeah, that would make sense." Tony could see that Deirdre's eyelids were at half-mast. He said, "Hey, you just woke up. I was just going to drop off the flowers and go, and then I thought I'd wait a few minutes to see if you woke up…"

Deirdre yawned and asked, "How long have you been waiting?"

Tony looked at the clock. He thought, *"Three hundred and seventeen minutes."* but said, "Not long. I should probably let you get some sleep."

"No, that's okay. I'll just lay here. You keep talking. Did you go out with any of these girls after the prom?"

"Nah, I just played prince charming for a night. It's easy to play prince charming for one night."

"What do you mean?"

"I don't know…" Tony looked up at the ceiling in concentration. "It seems that some girls, some women look at me… that they're not looking at me with their own eyes. It seems like they're looking at me with their girlfriend's eyes. Do you know what I mean? It's like I'm being judged as to whether or not I'd meet their girlfriend's approval. That probably sounds wicked vain. Maybe I'm not putting it right… let me back up…" Tony felt his face grow red with embarrassment. He thought, *"Smooth Tony, really smooth."*

Deirdre nodded and said, "No, I think I know what you mean. Some people just want to be with someone, and they don't care to get to know them."

"Exactly! They could go out on a date with a

mannequin."

Deirdre finished his sentence, "And they wouldn't know the difference."

Tony relaxed, grateful that the awkwardness was dispelled. They shared a smile and Deirdre asked, "So, did you always want to be a cop?"

"Actually, I wanted to be a barber."

Deirdre looked incredulous, "A barber? I don't know if I could see you as a barber."

"Well, when I was a kid, we'd go down to this Italian barbershop. There were three barbers there and they spoke Italian most of the time. The head barber was the owner and he was in charge. There were rules in his barbershop: there was no swearing, not ever, and everyone treated each other with respect, the barbers and the customers. The men acted like gentlemen. That barbershop was the way the whole world should be. There was nice Italian music playing on the radio: Frank Sinatra and Dean Martin. There was one song, and every time it would come on, everyone would go all quiet. Tony sang softly,

"Labbra come il vino
Gli occhi come il sole
Sto sognando ?

Labbra come il vino
Gli occhi come il sole
Lei sarà mia,
Sii mio"

I know it sounds wicked corny, but when you were sitting in the barber chair and the sun was coming in through the windows, it made you feel really special, like you were part of an elite group of men. It didn't matter if you were 12 years old, or 20 years old.

The head barber, Mr. Benevento, would tell me stories about my grandfather. Sometimes he'd teach me how to say things in Italian. One day I came in and Mr. Benevento was sitting in the Barber chair. I grabbed the… What's the name of the thing you put over someone, so they don't get hair all over themselves?"

"A cape."

"So I grabbed a cape, swung it over his head like he would do, and said, "Mr. Benevento, now I'm going to cut *your* hair." He laughed and laughed."

Deirdre lay her head back on her pillow and let Tony's words wash over her. It was comforting to have him here. He took her hand gently and talked of the things that made him feel good. Some people would probably call Tony old fashioned, but that was okay. His ideals might be old fashioned and romantic, but that set him apart from all the "other guys". The way he spoke to her, there in that dim hospital room, it wasn't so much the words he said, it was the way he said them; with his tone, with his eyes, it was as if he were saying much, much, more… as if he were saying, "It's alright. I'm here. I've got you. You're safe with me." And when he gently rubbed the back of her hand with his thumb, he was saying, "You're beautiful." Deirdre hadn't had a "man in her life" for a long time. When she compared any of the guys she'd ever dated to Tony, she felt she had never before had a man in her life at all. She could feel the walls that she had built up over the years crumbling. Walls she didn't even know she had made. She had become very independent and strong and felt good about that, but letting her guard down didn't seem like a weakness, not with Tony. Deirdre breathed in deeply and listened to his beautiful voice.

"All the barbers grew up in Italy and they would tell stories to whoever was sitting in their chair. Everyone would listen and pretend they weren't. One barber, Pasquale, grew up in Southern Italy. I guess it's pretty tough there. On the winding roads in the mountains, there are still bandits that'll stop cars at machinegun point and rob people. If the people don't cooperate, they'll just push their car right off the cliff. Now the police carry machineguns too." Tony could see that Deirdre was starting to fall asleep. "Oh, I hope you don't mind, your phone was ringing off the hook, and I didn't want it to wake you, so I answered it. Your friend Courtney called, and wants you to call her when you're "back in the world of the living." Visiting hours have been over for a while, but she'll be here first thing in the morning to see you."

Deirdre lay her head back on her pillow, "I'll call her in a little bit," she yawned and said, "I'd rather not, but I think I'm going to fall back asleep. I'm glad you came by. Oh, and you sing nice."

Tony blushed and gave her hand a squeeze, "Thanks," and as Deirdre fell back asleep, he quietly went out the door.

Chapter 10
A little visitor

Deirdre sat in bed reading. Without taking her eyes from her book, she felt along the table top, her fingers feeling through the empty Jell-O cups for a full one. Glancing up, she let out a little shriek, "Oh!" Standing in front of her was a little girl. The skin on one side of the girl's face was tight, shiny, and pink. Her hair poking through the openings of the gauze bandages on her head gave her the look of a dandelion. It was obvious to Deirdre that she'd been burned. Deirdre blushed, embarrassed by her reaction. Her heart dropped into her chest and she thought, *"Oh, God... the poor thing."* With an effort, she pulled her face into a smile and said, "You startled me. You're so quiet."

The girl's eyes narrowed, unconvinced. She turned to the door and said, "I know. I'm scary."

Deirdre said, "No! You're just so quiet, you startled me. Really. You're like a ninja."

The little girl stopped smiled at that. "I'm Sarah. What's your name?"

"I'm Deirdre. Nice to meet you, Sarah." Deirdre's legs were uncovered and Sarah looked with interest at the metal rod through her leg.

"Why do you have metal in your leg?"

"I was in an accident. I was riding my bike and... I got hurt."

Sarah's eyebrows shot up at that, "Wow! The most I've ever gotten riding my bike is a scraped elbow. They didn't have to put metal in my arm though."

"Well, that's good."

Sarah had a delightfully strong Southern accent, and looked to be eight or nine years old. Deirdre glanced out the door to see if anyone was accompanying her. The hall just outside her room was deserted. "Does anyone know you're here? Aren't you supposed to be in your room?"

Sarah hopped up and sat on the edge of Deirdre's bed. "It's okay. I'll go back soon. They know I like to walk around."

Deirdre was curious, "How long have you been in the hospital?"

"Months. There's not much to do here, so sometimes I walk. Sometimes I go to the cafeteria, and they give me pudding and cake, and sometimes I ride the elevator."

Deirdre marveled at this young girl and her courage. Three months in the hospital and she acted like any other little kid would. Well, a lot braver than any other little kid. "That sounds like fun. I like elevators, too."

"Do you have any friends in the hospital, Deirdre?"

"Other patients you mean? No." Deirdre looked down at the rod in her leg and said, "I don't get to move around like you. You're lucky."

Sarah patted Deirdre on the arm, "I can come and visit you if you want. We could be friends."

Deirdre smiled, "That sounds nice, Sarah. I'd like that."

Sarah looked down at her feet, "I used to visit my friend, Billy. Sometimes at night, I'd sneak over to his bed and we'd talk. He was my friend, but he's not here anymore."

Deirdre wasn't sure she wanted to know what "not here" meant. "What about your mom and dad? They visit you, right?"

Sarah looked at her feet and shook her head, "They're not allowed."

Deirdre wondered why parents wouldn't be allowed to visit their child, but thought it would be tactless to ask, so she said, "Both my parents don't visit me, either."

"Why not. What did *they* do?"

"They didn't do anything. They're just… They're really busy."

Sarah swung her legs back and forth and said, "That's too bad. You must miss your mom. I miss my mom."

Deirdre and Sarah were interrupted by a knock on the

doorframe. A nurse poked her head in the door and said with relief, "There you are Sarah. I've been looking all over for you." The nurse exchanged a look with Deirdre and looked back to Sarah, "It's time for your bath young lady."

Sarah frowned, "Oh come on. Just a few more minutes, please?"

The nurse shook her head, "I'm sorry sweetie, but it's time to go."

Sarah hopped off the bed and turned to Deirdre, "Can I visit you another time?"

"Sure, Sarah, any time."

Sarah started to leave with the nurse, then ran back and took Deirdre by the hand, "We're friends now, right?"

Deirdre nodded, "We're friends, absolutely."

"Okay, but... Could you not tell anyone? If my mom finds out she might not want us to be friends."

"I won't tell anyone. I promise."

"You swear?"

Deirdre made an X over her heart with her index finger, "Cross my heart, and hope to die."

Sarah smiled and left with the nurse.

Chapter 11
Beacon Street

Captain Rodriguez opened his glass office door and ushered the detectives inside, "Detective Sullivan, Detective Capella, this is Donald Miller."

Awaiting them was a well-dressed man in his upper 40's.

"*Rich dude*," thought Tony. "*Ticked off rich dude.*"

Capt. Rodriguez said, "Take a seat, Mr. Miller."

"I'll stand thank you. My baby girl's lying in the city morgue, and I'd like to know what the hell you're going to do about it."

Capt. Rodriguez put his hands on his desk and took a deep breath. The Captain said, "I'm sorry for your loss, Mr. Miller, but I'm not sure there's any more we can do. The autopsy report states that your daughter died from a heart attack. The attending physician signed off the death certificate and, since you expressed concern, the Medical Examiner as well as the Coroner were called in, and corroborated his findings. I'm sorry for your loss, but I don't see that there is anything to investigate."

"My daughter was alive and perfectly healthy the day before she died. I don't buy this bull that my baby girl died of a heart attack. My daughter has a personal trainer. She was 25 years old, did cardio three times a week, and you think walking two blocks is going to kill her? Bull. I'm a very influential man, Captain." Mr. Miller walked over and put his face inches from the Captain's, "I don't know how you do things around here, but what I do know is that if you don't get on the stick, and find out what happened to my daughter, the mayor will hear about it."

Capt. Rodriguez looked calm, but Tony noticed the tendon standing out in his neck. Capt. Rodriguez said,

"Yes, I had a call from the Mayor this morning. I'll just turn you over to Detectives Sullivan and Capella."

Tony motioned to the door, "If you'll just come this way Sir, we'll need to ask you some questions."

Mr. Miller looked at Tony, cocked his head to one side and said, "Do I know you?"

"I don't believe so, Sir."

Mr. Miller's hands were balled into fists, "You can come to my house." He looked at Capt. Rodriguez, "I don't like the smell in here. Here's my card. 2 o'clock."

And with that, Donald Miller thrust a business card into Sully's hand, turned on his heel, and walked out of the police station.

Tony and Sully walked back to their desks. Sully squeezed his bulk behind his desk, flopped back in his chair, and put his hands behind his head.

"All right kid, you see what you can run down on Mr. Congeniality's daughter. You can head over to the hospital for the coroner's report and medical records. That should give you plenty of time to meet Miller at... 1330 Beacon Street at 2:00."

Tony's jaw dropped, "Wait. What? We just get a case dumped in our laps and you want me to-"

Sully held up a hand to silence him. "You need to get your feet wet, Tony. So you're off to the hospital and to meet Miller. This is my training program. I say jump, you ask how high."

"Okaaay, and what'll you be doing?"

Sully pulled a ham sandwich and a bag of chips from his desk drawer and said, "Eatin' lunch."

"Terrific."

"Go get 'em, Tiger."

A half hour later, Tony flashed his badge at the hospital CEO. *"That never gets old."* he thought. "Hello Mr. Green. I'm Detective Capella. I've got a few questions to ask you."

Frank Green was the quintessential CEO: perfect hair with just a touch of gray, $2,000 suit, striped tie and a freshly pressed shirt. Tony could tell what he was going to say before he even said it. "I'm a very-"

"Busy man," Tony finished. "I know. I'm pretty busy myself. It's just a minute of your time, Mr. Green, and I'll be out of your hair."

"All right, all right. Go ahead."

"I need access to the medical records and death certificate of a Miss Nancy Miller. She died this past Monday in the emergency room." Tony handed over a form requiring the documents.

"What are you bothering me for? You could have gone to my head of records. As I say, I'm a very busy man."

If Tony's martial arts training taught him anything it was how to read a face and body language. *Is it just me, or is this guy sweating gumballs?* "I did see the head of records, but it seems everyone is HIPAA crazy around here. She sent me to you."

Mr. Green pulled out a piece of stationary and scratched off a note. "Give this to my secretary and she'll set it up with our medical records department. Goodbye Detective."

Tony stopped for a cup of coffee and to look over Nancy Miller's medical records, before he had to meet Mr. Miller on Beacon Street. He looked over the information he had gathered so far and thought, *"Nothin'."* Nancy Miller's tox-screen was negative. The only chemicals they found in her blood was a low-level of caffeine and the medications she'd received in the Emergency Room before her death. No drugs, no alcohol: nothing. Cause of death: heart attack due to heart defect. Tony shrugged his shoulders and muttered, "I can see Capt. Rodriguez's point. Maybe there isn't anything to investigate."

Tony put the medical records back in their envelope and headed out to meet Mr. Miller.

Beacon Street, home of the brownstone, where all the women are blonde, have the same haircut, and go horseback riding on the weekends. Tony parked his Jeep and walked up the worn granite steps to the centuries old brick building.

Before his hand reached the knocker, Mr. Miller's voice came over the intercom, "It's unlocked. Come in."

Brownstones were usually grand, but this took the cake. Tony's eyes followed the curve of the wrought iron railing up and up.

"It's nice isn't it? One brownstone was too small, so I bought two and had them joined so Nancy would have more room. Come Detective; let's go talk in the study." Tony followed Mr. Miller into a wood paneled room with red leather chairs. "Sit down, please. Where's your partner? Sullivan right?"

"He's running down some leads." Tony pulled out his phone, "Do you mind if I record this? I need to ask you some questions."

"Ask away."

Tony hesitated, "You understand, Mr. Miller, I have to ask you… Was your daughter a drug user?"

"My Nancy never did drugs. Maybe a little pot in college, but that's it."

"Are any of her friends, boyfriends, drug users?"

"No, absolutely not. Nancy is… Nancy *was* a good girl. She was going places. Her body was her temple. She wouldn't have anything to do with drugs."

"Did she have a boyfriend, somebody close?"

"She'd get dressed up on a Saturday night once in a while and go out with her girlfriends. But no, she didn't have a boyfriend. Not since college. The only one Nancy spent a considerable amount of time with was her friend Beth. Beth Connors. She'd drag Nancy out to her country

club, or to some garden party. Long time friends, they
went to school together."

"I'd like Beth Connors address, if I may."

"I'll make sure you get it. Nancy was very focused on
her career, that and shopping. She must have 300 pairs of
shoes."

"May I see her bedroom?"

Mr. Miller stood, "Up the stairs, I'll show you."

The first thing in the bedroom that caught the eye was
an enormous canopy bed with dark-wood posts, carved in
the form of cherubs holding hands. Nancy's bedroom
looked much like any other young woman's, except more
grand. The bureau was covered with makeup and lipsticks.
Posters covered the walls, mostly of giraffes. There were
stuffed animal giraffes as well, including one in the corner
that was 5 feet tall.

"Giraffes, huh, my sister's into unicorns." Tony picked
up a group picture of cheerleaders and wasn't surprised to
see Nancy front and center. He put the picture down, "I
understand she passed out at work. Did she socialize with
any of her co-workers? "

"Not that I know of. I don't believe so. I'm a busy man.
I don't... I didn't get to spend as much time with my
daughter as I would have liked."

"Would you know of anyone who would wish you, or
your daughter harm?"

"I make a lot of money, and I step on a lot of toes, but
not hard enough for anyone to want me or my daughter
dead."

Tony nodded, "Do you mind if I take a closer look
around?"

"No. You go right ahead. I'll be downstairs when you're
through."

Tony couldn't believe that Sully sent him here on his
own. *"He's supposed to be training me."* He thought as he
poked through drawers filled with socks and underwear.

"What if I miss something? What if I make a complete mess of this?"

Tony had plenty of experience searching for hidden drugs. He thought he'd use that experience in looking for anything that might help him figure out how Mr. Miller's daughter died. *"Maybe this is some kind of detective initiation... But Sully wouldn't do that to me. Would he?"*

He looked under the mattress, in the toes of shoes, and there were 57 pair, in jewelry boxes, even in the hanging light fixture. He found some old letters, and sat on the edge of the bed to read through them. Most talked about ski trips and country club parties, but the letters had one thing in common. They painted a picture of Nancy as a kind, caring person. As he opened a letter, a photograph fell to the floor. It was a picture of Nancy with a group of smiling friends, in cap and gown, after their college graduation ceremony. He ran a hand over his face and thought, *"She's just a girl; an all American kid with a bright future. Damn."*

Tony's face turned red when he found a picture of Nancy and her friends skinny-dipping. It was nothing bad. In fact it had sort of a Norman Rockwell quality. Tony was afraid that he might find something unseemly; something that Nancy's father would find and be hurt by. He was grateful that he didn't find anything like that. He was also frustrated that he didn't find anything to help him with the case.

Tony snapped a few pictures of Nancy's room in case he needed to refresh his memory later and looked again at Nancy's bureau. He walked over and picked up a jar of makeup remover. He unscrewed the cap and took a sniff. He thought, *"It's a long-shot..."* He put down the jar, and made his way down the curving staircase.

Waiting at the bottom of the stairs was Donald Miller, who said, "I'm putting this place on the market. I can't stand to be here by myself. Not without my Nancy."

"Do you have any other family, Mr. Miller?"

Donald Miller's eyes narrowed, "The only family I have are interested in one thing and that's my money." Mr. Miller stared off into space. His look of anger changed to one of intense thought, "I do have an uncle and some cousins in Scotland. I've never met them. My father and my uncle, Angus, had a falling out before I was born." He seemed to be talking more to himself than to Tony, "They've been salmon farmers for generations. When I was young, I used to dream about running away to the Highlands and becoming a salmon farmer."

Tony tried to picture this well-dressed businessman dressed in a kilt, farming salmon. Tony thought, *"He'd probably quadruple their business."*

It seemed that Mr. Miller was picturing the same thing. He came out of his daydream with a start, turned to Tony and said, "Hey, you look so young. How long have you been a detective? This isn't your first day is it?"

Tony thought *"first week."* but said, "Long enough. Oh, and I'd like to send someone by to pick up your daughter's makeup and beauty supplies. It's a long-shot, but maybe the guys in the lab will find something that's not supposed to be there."

Mr. Miller nodded, "Sure, no problem... Hey, I know where I've seen you before... on television. You're the one who stopped the terrorists from gassing the T."

"Yeah, that's me." Tony looked up the staircase, in the direction of Nancy's room, and thought, *"She's just a girl who likes giraffes, or she was."* He shook Mr. Miller's hand and said, "Mr. Miller, I assure you, if there was any foul play in the death of your daughter, I'll do my utmost to bring those responsible to justice."

Mr. Miller bowed his head for a moment before saying, "That's all I'm asking, Detective."

Chapter 12
Strictly professional

Sully took another bite of his egg-muffin and put it down on the dashboard, so he could take another swig of coffee. Tony grimaced and said, "How can you eat that stuff first thing in the morning? That stuff's gonna' kill ya'."

"Breakfast of champions, kid, breakfast of champions."

"More like breakfast of heart disease, and will you stop calling me 'kid'?"

"Comes with the new badge, kid." Sully hit a pothole and reached up to save his sandwich.

"You move pretty fast for an old dude. Too bad you're not that fast on the gun range."

Sully wedged his sandwich more firmly between the dashboard and the windshield and said, "Pfff! You beat me what? Twice? I wouldn't let it go to your head."

"Try three times. You're just that much too slow."

"When you use a 45 you're bound to be a little slower than with your 9 mm pea-shooter."

"Come on Sully, everybody uses a 9 mm now: swat, tac-ops, Secret Service. The only people that carry a 45 are hunting grizzly bears."

"Well, if we run into a grizzly bear we'll be prepared, won't we? Plus, a 45'll shoot right through a 2 X 4, or a cinderblock, or a windshield... where that wussy 9 mm round will spend itself on the sheet rock."

"Yeah, it's supposed to. That way, if you're shooting at someone in an apartment building, the round doesn't go through the wall and kill some lady making spaghetti."

"That's why I don't miss." Sully switched lanes and asked, "How's that Irish girl in the hospital doing? I heard you went to see her again."

Tony's jaw dropped, "How do you know that?"

Sully gave Tony a wink and said, "A little birdie told me they saw you with flowers in the hospital, and I put two and two together."

"Does this little birdie have a name?"

"Hutchinson. Come on Tony, you know everyone in the Boston P.D. knows everything about everyone. We gotta look out for each other, how are we gonna' do that if we don't know what's going on?"

Tony shook his head, "Yeah, I guess..." That was true as far as it went. Everybody did seem to know what was going on with everybody else, down to how much sugar they put in their coffee.

Sully pulled up to a red light and said, "So, tell me about this girl. Are you two an item or what?"

Tony scratched his neck, "An item? I mean, I really only just met her... She is cool though."

Sully asked, "Cool like leather jacket, motorcycle riding cool?"

Tony said, "No she's like... she's not like a poser... she's like 'I'm me and that's it' kind of cool."

Sully nodded and said, "That's cool."

Sully did a U-turn and pulled up in front of Whitney and Brown law offices, "Alright kid, when we go in there, you do all the talking."

Tony stopped dead and looked at Sully, "I'm gonna' do all the talkin'? I thought I was supposed to "learn from your experience".

"Sully put his hand on Tony's shoulder and said, "When I was a kid, my old man threw me in the water to teach me how to swim. Now I'm throwin' you in. So learn how to swim."

"You know they do have swimming lessons now right? Is that why you had me go solo to talk to Miller? Who's my partner anyway? You or your old man?"

"That would be me. Till death do us part, or retirement, or disability or layoffs... or me winning the lottery..."

Tony walked through the revolving door, while Sully went through a regular hinged one. When they entered the foyer Sully said, "Lesson one, grasshopper: don't go through revolving doors, makes it a bit hard to get behind cover. Hey, I should call you grasshopper from now on, with you're being a karate man."

"You can call me anything you want, Sully, that doesn't mean I'm going to answer to it."

"Touché kid."

They took the elevator to the 21st floor, and walked up to a receptionist with a Bluetooth in her ear. Sully motioned Tony forward with a grand wave of his hand, "Time to swim little fishy."

Tony pulled out his badge, "Good morning. I'm Detective Capella and this is Detective Sullivan. We're here to see Mr. Harold Ross.

The receptionist looked up at Tony, who couldn't see her eyes, only the image of her computer screen reflected in her glasses, and said, "One moment." She touched a button on her keyboard and spoke into her microphone, "Mr. Ross, I have detectives Capella and Sullivan here to see you." She looked to Tony and said, "You may go right in."

"Thanks."

Harold Ross was not what Tony expected. Instead of a plush office, Tony saw that Mr. Ross sat behind an old, utilitarian steel desk, with a crank pencil sharpener mounted to it. Filing cabinets lined two walls. Broad in the shoulder and thin-waisted, his white hair cropped short, Mr. Ross sat scrutinizing a folder, his sleeves rolled up to the elbow. When Tony and Sully entered, Mr. Ross got out from behind his desk, walked over and shook their hands, "Detectives, what can I do for you today."

"Firm grip. I hope I look that good when I'm his age." thought Tony. *"This guy's got 10 years on Sully and could*

probably do laps around him. He looks more like a fitness instructor than a businessman."

Mr. Ross smiled affably at the detectives.

Tony said, "I'd like to ask you some questions about your former employee, Nancy Miller."

"Miller, right. Let me see." Mr. Ross walked over to a filing cabinet and pulled out a manila folder. He opened it and read standing, "Yes, Nancy Miller... excellent worker, all positive reviews. It's a shame when a young person passes... Never missed a day, secretary to one of our partners, Daniel Whitcomb."

Tony said, "Perhaps we should be speaking with Mr. Whitcomb."

"Hold on." Mr. Ross pressed his intercom, "Linda, would you ask Daniel Whitcomb to step into my office please? Thank you." Mr. Ross released the button, "He'll be right in. Might I ask what this is all about? Do you expect foul play?"

"We're investigating the death of one of your employees. A young lady who was apparently healthy one minute, and an hour later, she was dead."

Mr. Ross returned to his seat behind the desk. He steepled his fingers and said, "Our employees undergo rigorous background checks, family checks, drug testing, as well as psychological testing. Of course we'll cooperate fully Detective, but I believe you'll find you're barking up the wrong tree here."

Tony tapped his finger on the desktop and said, "I had a friend in high school. He cheated on tests all the time. He never got caught."

Tony turned as someone knocked on the door. A thin, blonde, middle-aged man in a blue suit came in. "Daniel, this is Detective Capella and Detective Sullivan. They're investigating the death of your secretary."

"Investigating? I was told she'd died from a heart attack."

Tony asked, "Mr. Whitcomb what can you tell me about Nancy Miller?"

"Nancy… very nice girl. Hard worker. Somewhat of an over achiever, to be frank." Daniel Whitcomb spoke with perfect diction, as if he were speaking to a large group of people, weighing every word before it passed his lips. "Always triple checked anything going out or coming in. I never had any reason to complain."

Tony found Mr. Whitcomb's tone somewhat disconcerting. He asked, "Did you see her on the morning of her death?"

"No. I came in about a half hour after she was taken by ambulance."

Tony asked, "What was your relationship with Miss Miller?"

Daniel Whitcomb put his hands on his hips and said, "My relationship? I was her boss."

"Did you ever see Miss Miller after work? Go out to lunch, that sort of thing?"

Daniel Whitcomb looked shocked, "What are you implying? No, my relationship with Nancy was strictly professional." Mr. Whitcomb turned to his boss, "Harold, you don't think I had anything to do with this, surely?"

Mr. Ross said, "Take it easy, Daniel. They're just doing their job."

Daniel Whitcomb frowned, looked back to Tony. Nostrils flared in agitation, he said, "My partner and I are very happy, and, as I said, my relationship with Nancy was strictly professional."

Daniel's statement was met with a stony silence by the detectives, and Mr. Ross.

Daniel looked from one face to the other, took a deep breath, and in a more affable voice said, "I liked Nancy as a person. She was attentive to detail, not easily ruffled, and…" his face reddened slightly, "She caught a mistake or two of mine that the average secretary would surely have missed. And she brought them to my attention discreetly, and with a degree of tact for which I was most grateful."

Tony asked, "Did she have any relations with anyone else in your office that you are aware of?"

"Not that I know of. She rarely mentioned her personal life. Nancy was a very attractive woman. The young men would walk by just to get a glimpse of her. Some mornings it was like a parade. There was one though... one who spent more time than the others hanging around her desk. Bill Matthews. His office was down the hall from Nancy's. If you believe water cooler gossip, he fancies himself quite the lady's man. He seemed quite smitten with Nancy."

Tony turned to Mr. Ross, "Could we see this Bill Matthews?"

Again, Mr. Ross tapped his intercom. "Linda, would you ask Bill Matthews to step into my office?"

Linda's voice came over the speaker, "I'm sorry, Mr. Ross. It seems Bill Matthews is not in today."

"Not in?"

"He called in sick."

Mr. Ross looked thoughtful, then rifled through some of the folders on his desk. He opened one and ran his finger down a column, "Ah, yes. I've been meaning to speak to Bill about some of the expenses he's been charging on his company account: dinners, hotel rooms, entertainment, the list goes on."

Tony exchanged a glance with Sully and said, "Mr. Ross, I'd like Bill Matthew's address."

Chapter 13
Good Advice

Deirdre was staring at a half finished sudoku puzzle when she heard a gentle rapping on her door-jamb. A nurse steeped inside and said, "Hi Deirdre, I'm Judy, Sarah's nurse."

Judy was young, dressed in pink scrubs covered in kittens, and a matching pink stethoscope about her neck. Beneath her bright smile, Deirdre saw, in the young nurse's eyes, intelligence and caring that belied her years and puerile attire. Judy said, "I just wanted to drop by and tell you that you might have a visitor today, and to make sure that it's okay with you."

Deirdre sat up, "It's okay with me. I mean, I'm not going anywhere, and I enjoy Sarah's company."

"I'm glad. Sarah doesn't have many visitors."

"Sarah told me that her mother's not allowed to visit. Can you tell me why?"

Judy sighed and said, "It's not like it's a secret, but if you wouldn't mention it to Sarah..."

"Of course not."

"Sarah's mother is a real... naturalist. She's totally wrapped up in holistic medicine. If Sarah's uncle hadn't brought her in after she was burned, I doubt she'd even be in the hospital. Her mother would probably be treating her horrible burns at home."

Deirdre nodded in understanding, "I've heard stories like that. I heard one kid died from being constipated. His parents kept him at home, when the hospital could've straightened him out in about two seconds."

Judy pulled up a chair next to Deirdre and sat down, "It's lucky Sarah's alive. Her mother came in one day, and one of the candy stripers caught her trying to put honey all over Sarah's new skin grafts. It was a nightmare. Thank God it didn't do more damage."

Deirdre looked horrified, "Honey? Why would she do that?"

Judy rolled her eyes and said, "It's supposed to be a natural remedy for burns. Minor burns, maybe, but not for 3rd degree."

"How did you get the honey off?"

"We poured Luke-warm water slowly over the honey and dissolved it. We only lost a small amount of grafted skin. It could've been much, much worse."

"Did they arrest Sarah's mother?"

"They had to carry her out kicking and screaming."

Deirdre pictured Sarah's mother and felt badly for her. She could imagine a woman who felt that what she was doing was the right thing, and was so convinced that she would be willing to go to jail for it. Deirdre felt badly for Sarah's mother, but she didn't agree with her. She asked Judy, "So, is she in jail?"

Judy shook her head, "No, but there's a court order that says she can't come within 100 feet of the hospital."

"What about Sarah's father?"

"He tussled with one of the security guards, so the same goes for him. Only the uncle visits from time to time."

Deirdre shook her head, "Poor kid. It's rotten when kids have to suffer for their parent's behavior. How much longer will she be in the hospital?"

Judy ran her hands over her face, "She still has quite a way to go. Skin grafting's come along way, but it still takes time." She stood up and asked, "You sure it's okay for Sarah to come and visit? If it's not, just tell me and I'll work it out."

"It's fine, really." Deirdre ran her finger over the metal rod in her leg and said, "I thought this was bad. That little girl sure put things in perspective. You send her right over."

Judy left, and 10 minutes later Sarah walked in the door with two ice cream sandwiches and a bag of pretzels. Sarah took her place on the side of Deirdre's bed and said, "Hi

Deirdre." and gave Deirdre a hug, which she returned.

"Hi Sarah. I'm glad you came to visit."

"Me too. I know what it's like to be stuck in a bed. When I first got to the hospital they wouldn't let me move at all. I was good though. I didn't touch my new skin. Not too much anyway."

"That's good."

"The doctors told me I'm the best patient they've ever had."

"I'll bet. That must have been very… I mean…"

Sarah nodded sagely and said, "It's ok. When I grow up I'm going to be a doctor, or maybe a nurse."

"That sounds nice. I wonder what I'll be when I grow up."

"But you are grown up!"

"Yeah, well… I was a bike messenger before I… before the hospital. Before that I sat behind a computer. I'm not sure what I'll do when I get out of here."

Sarah pursed her lips in thought before saying, "You can be whatever you want."

Deirdre guffawed and said, "That would be nice."

Sarah frowned. "I'm not joking!"

Deirdre was taken-a-back. She said, "I didn't mean, um…"

"You CAN be what ever you want. Ok, maybe not an astronaut but you can do something you like to do. You're nice. You could be a teacher. You'd be a good teacher."

"You think so?"

"You could be my teacher."

Judy walked into the room and said brightly, "Hi Sarah. Time to go."

Sarah's jaw dropped, she looked at Judy and said, "Oh, come on!"

Judy looked down at Sarah and said, "I'm sorry Sarah, but the doctor's waiting. You know we can't make him wait."

Deirdre patted Sarah's hand and said, "It's okay, Sarah. You can come back anytime."

"Is that a promise?"

"It's a promise."

Chapter 14
Why are the police here to see you?

Tony and Sully drove down Main Street in Hingham. They passed one big beautiful old house after another, each looking more like a mansion than the last. They also passed lots of women up and down the sidewalk either walking dogs, jogging, or pushing a baby stroller. There were no men, only women. "Gee, does anyone in this town work?" Tony asked.

Sully laughed, "The guys work. They work their butts off to buy their wives these houses and their SUVs, so that when they get divorced their wives boyfriends will have a nice place to live."

Tony snorted, "Nice Sully, but it all can't be the same. This must be the rich part of town."

Sully crushed his candy bar wrapper and tossed it in the back seat, "I knew this one guy, a doctor, he told me that his wife has been to every pyramid in the world: Egypt, Machu Picchu, I think that one's in South America. She was looking for "pyramid power", and this poor sap's putting in 14 hour days to pay for this crap."

Tony learned early on not to bring up divorce with Sully. That subject was good for hours, and almost always ended up rich woman bashing. "Your wife's cool." Tony said.

"My wife's from Dorchester. She's tough. She works for a living. Not like these prima donnas."

As they drove, Tony took in the big houses with their manicured lawns, wrought iron fences, old maples and oaks and said, "It's a nice town though."

Sully rolled his eyes. "Yeah, real nice. There's this one street in Hingham, real pretty street, where there used to be this pesticide factory, back in like the 1930s. Back then they didn't have regulations. So this place gets torn down and nobody thinks about it anymore. And here we are now, years and years later, and all these people within half a mile from where the factory was start dying of cancer. They call it cancer alley."

Tony frowned, "Did they do anything about it?"

"Nah, it's a nice town, it's a nice street. Wouldn't want the property values to go down. If it happened in another town, they would have treated it like Three Mile Island and closed it all off, but nobody talks about it. Maybe they figure if they don't, it'll just go away."

"That's pretty screwed up."

"Yup."

Sully pulled down a cul-de-sac, "Here it is. The beautiful home of William Matthews." Above the doors of the two-car garage was a dark blue sign with "Matthews" carved in it, the lettering painted white.

As Tony and Sully got out of the car, Tony asked, "Do you want me to do all the talking with this guy, too?"

"Gotta swim, little fishy. Gotta' swim."

They walked up the brick walkway, bordered by two rows of topiaries that looked, to Tony, just like cork screws, and up the steps to the two-story house. Tony rang the bell and gave a couple wraps on the clapboards. A woman in her mid-40's opened the door. She took in their suits, said, "I'm already a Christian," and started to close the door in their faces.

Tony put his palm on the door and cleared his throat, "Yeah, me too, ma'am, but that's not why we're here." Tony pulled out his badge and made a mental note to have his badge ready before he knocked in the future. Sometimes he forgot that he wasn't wearing a police uniform anymore. "I'm Detective Capella, and this is Detective Sullivan. Is Mr. Matthews home?"

Mrs. Matthews opened stood in the doorway: blonde shoulder length hair, gold hoop earrings, pants cut just below the knee, and a look of strong displeasure. She asked, "What is this about?"

"We just have a few questions for your husband,

ma'am."

Mrs. Matthews called over her shoulder, "Bill! The police are here to see you. Why are the police here to see you?"

Bill Matthews came to the front door in a fluffy white bathrobe with a gold emblem from one of the more expensive hotels, his nose red and the corners of his eyes filled with gunk, "What is it? What do you want?"

"Just a few questions, Mr. Matthews. May we come inside?"

"Okay, okay come in." Bill Matthews walked them into the living room, which was full of new "wood like" furniture, heavy drapes and gaudy lamps. It looked like the decorator had tried for the Newport Mansion look, but had missed the mark. Bill Matthews motioned them to the couch and asked, "Would you like to sit down?"

"Thank you." Tony and Sully sat on the oversized sofa, while Bill took a seat in a winged armchair.

"Honey, why don't you, um…"

Mrs. Matthews put her fists on her hips and looked down angrily at her husband, "I'm staying right here, Bill."

Sully gave Tony a look that said, *"Ya' see what I mean?"*

Tony agreed with Sully. "Mr. Matthews, we're investigating the death of one of your coworkers, Miss Nancy Miller. Could you tell me what your relationship was with Miss Miller?"

Bill Mathews looked decidedly uncomfortable. He looked down at the back of his hands and a flush crept up is neck. That's when Mrs. Matthews went ballistic, "I knew it! I knew it! You've been cheating on me! My sisters all said you were no good!"

Tony got up to separate Mrs. Matthews from Mr. Matthews, who had curled up in a ball on the chair as Mrs. Matthews ineffectually punched and slapped him.

When Tony finally got them apart, Sully said, "Tony, why don't you take Mrs. Matthews into the kitchen? I think she needs to calm down a little bit."

Tony took Mrs. Matthews by the arm and guided her into the kitchen. He eased her into chair at the kitchen table and sat himself down on a stool. Mrs. Matthews put her palms down flat on the table and gazed out the window, her eyes unfocused. "That's it, I'm done. The kids are old enough now. I'm done."

Tony didn't know what to say. He could hear Sully and Mr. Matthews in the living room. "What do you mean? I just worked down the hall from Nancy, so did a lot of other guys. Are you interviewing them?"

Sully didn't raise his voice, "No. I'm interviewing you." Sully got up from the couch, walked over and looked down at Bill Matthews and said, "I just had a little chat with Nancy's boss. He seems to think that you had it bad for Nancy Miller... real bad."

"Me? No. I'm a happily married man... I mean..."

Sully continued, "And a little bird told me that you've been misusing your expense account; Hotels? Entertainment? And what kind of entertainment would that be, Mr. Matthews? When I look up the receipts from your charges I'm willing to bet it was the female type of entertainment. I pulled your file this morning. You've been arrested..." Sully looked at his notepad "twice for solicitation."

Bill Matthews cringed and pleaded, "Keep it down, will you? That was a long time ago. If my wife knew..."

"Now, we can do this here, or we can do it at the station. You might look a little silly sitting in a cell with a bunch of other guys wearing that fluffy bathrobe. Let's try it again. What was your relationship with Miss Miller?"

Bill Matthews put his face in his hands and said, "Nothing ever happened between me and Nancy. I mean, she was hot, but we never did anything. I mean, I wanted to, but no, we never did anything. She totally shot me down."

In the kitchen Mrs. Matthews looked up at Tony and

asked, "You wouldn't happen to know the name of a good divorce lawyer, would you Detective?" Tony shook his head, "No ma'am. I'm sorry."

Sully, hands on his hips, looked down at Mr. Matthews and asked, "Do you have any objection to giving a DNA sample?"

"No objection at all. I may not be, that is, I have my vices, Detective. But I'm not a killer."

"Would you take a lie detector test, Mr. Matthews?"

"Yes. Yes I would."

As Tony walked from the kitchen into the living room, Sully said, "We'll be in touch, Mr. Matthews. Don't leave town."

Back in the car, Tony said, "I heard you ask miller if he'd give a DNA sample and a lie detector test. What was that about?"

"I wanted to see what his reaction would be. What do you think, Tony? Ya' think Bill Matthews is a killer?"

"He's a grade-A creep, but a killer? He has a record for solicitation. Anything else?"

"Nothing."

"I wouldn't count him out completely, but my gut tells me he's telling the truth."

Sully pulled the car onto the highway. "So, what's are next move, Tony?"

"Well..." Tony looked out the car window and said, "Besides her father, the closest person to Nancy Miller is her best friend, Beth Connors. First thing tomorrow, I say we pay her a visit."

Chapter 15
I'd like that a lot

"Go light; I'm going for the natural look. I want it to look like I'm not wearing makeup at all."

Courtney circled the brush in the makeup pallet, "I got you covered, Dee. Don't worry. I brought my whole arsenal with me."

The entire surface of the bed, that didn't include Deirdre, was covered with open makeup bags and cases. "What color eye shadow do you want? Ya' want blue? It'll bring out your eyes."

"No, I think that's too much, just a little tan. It'll look more natural."

"Ya' want the pearl, or the regular?"

"Just the regular, Court. Come On! I'm trying to look natural here!"

Courtney smiled mischievously. "Oooo, someone's getting a little hot under the collar. You must really like this guy."

Deirdre smiled. "I hardly know him. He seems really nice, I mean, really cool. I don't know... I like the way he looks at me."

Courtney twirled the brush in her fingertips. "It doesn't hurt that he's really hot. Does it?"

Deirdre looked up through half raised lids. "No, that doesn't hurt." She ran her fingers through her hair and grinned back at Courtney.

Courtney chuckled and said, "Okay, now a little lip-gloss and we're done. What'll it be? Pretty in Peach? Mohave Desert or Barely There?"

"Hmmmm, let's go Pretty in Peach."

"Too bad I didn't have time to give you a sponge bath. Bet your cop friend would have liked that!"

Tony had his hand raised to knock on the door frame, and stopped just in time. *"Yes, yes he would have liked that,"* he thought, as he felt his cheeks grow hot. He was psyched and embarrassed simultaneously. *"I'll just give them a few minutes."* He took a deep breath, turned around and headed for the cafeteria.

Tony watched from a hallway as Courtney passed. She looked like she was going on vacation, with makeup bags over her shoulders, under her arms, and in both hands. After she passed, Tony made his way to Deirdre's room. He knocked three times on the doorframe. "Hello? Deirdre?" Tony blushed at the memory of his last scrubbed entrance.

Deirdre checked herself once more in a compact mirror and said, "Hey, come on in."

"How ya' doin'?" Tony asked, as he pulled a chair close to her hospital bed.

"I'm doin'. I'm doin' doing better than I was."

Tony put two coffees down on the over-bed table. He opened his mouth, closed it, opened it again and said, "I almost asked you, 'What's new?' but that's probably not the smartest thing to ask someone who's in the hospital." He looked out the window at the gathering dusk and thought, *"Tony you idiot, get it together."* "Let me start over." He smiled. "You look really nice."

Deirdre returned his smile. "Thanks. That *is* much better than 'What's new?'"

"I think I saw your friend, Courtney, leaving."

"Yeah, she's great. She comes off as a real "wild child", but she's really a loving, caring person... a great friend. I met her in the beauty shop. She was cutting my hair, and we got to talking. She told me how she had caught her boyfriend cheating on her. He denied it, but Court looked through the messages on his phone, and there were like 100."

"What did she do?"

"She threw his phone out the window, followed by his clothes, his TV, his Xbox, and his CD collection. She grabbed her cat, all her stuff, and left."

Tony laughed and said, "I can see her doing that."

"Courtney asked me if I knew of anyone looking for a roommate, and just like that, I decided that I'd had had enough of living with my family, and that it was time to make a change. I was like, "In Boston? An apartment in Boston?" A week later we had an apartment, with an air conditioner that sounds like it's full of gravel, a leak in the roof, and a neon sign from the movie theater across the street that lights the place up at night."

"I take it you like living in the city?"

"It's great. Everything's right there. If I want a bagel, I can walk down the stairs, take a right and walk into the bagel shop. Two doors down is Chinese food, where five bucks will buy dinner and a drink. Pizza, laundry, anything and everything is either within walking distance, a bike ride, or a quick ride on the T."

They looked at each other for a moment before Tony said, "This place must be getting to you. I wish I could take you out of here for an hour or two."

"Oh yeah? Where would you take me?"

Tony cocked his head to one side. "Hmmm, somewhere nice… Maybe the Gardner Museum."

Deirdre looked a little flustered. "A museum?"

"No, yeah, I mean, this place isn't like a museum. It's not all cold, and you don't have to whisper. There was this really wealthy woman, Isabella Gardner, who was really into art. They turned her house into a museum. It's exactly the same as it was when she lived there, furniture and everything. I guess that's why I like it. It's comfortable, and it feels like your visiting a friend at their house, I mean like, a really rich friend. Plus, the paintings there are awesome. The lighting's kind of dim, not like that harsh lighting at other museums, and there's a courtyard garden filled with flowers with a glass roof four stories up. It's really cool. I think you'll really like it."

"Sounds cool." Deirdre smiled mischievously and said, "Okay, we've been to the museum, so now where are you taking me?"

"Okay… now we're leaving the museum, and you take my arm as I walk you the car, and you tell me how cool the museum was, and how you liked the paintings, especially the one with the twirling Spanish dancers, and we drive to… no, not the movies… We drive to… Rhode Island."

"Rhode Island!? What's in Rhode Island?"

"Nothin', it's just a long drive."

Deirdre pursed her lips. "So, you want to go on a long drive with me?"

Tony put his elbow on his knee, his chin in his palm, and leaned closer. With a half smile, and dreamy eyes he said, "Yeah, I'd like that a lot."

"Me, too."

"So, what do you want to talk about on our long drive?

Tony said, "All sorts of things. Let's see… What was Deirdre like when she was a little girl?"

"I was a typical little girl. I had scraped knees, I chased my brothers around the house, caused mayhem; typical little girl stuff. How about you?"

"I was a typical little girl too."

Deirdre laughed and said, "Come on."

"OK, I'm the youngest so I got to do pretty much what I wanted. I, too, caused plenty of mayhem. I tried football but it really wasn't my thing. Karate was different."

"Ah, a karate master."

"Not hardly. Maybe when I'm a hundred."

"Do you still do it?"

"Whenever I can. When I was in blues it came in handy more than once, but it's more than that, it's good for the mind. It's good for the soul."

"That's how I feel on my bike. I feel free, weightless…"

"Yeah, karate's like that."

"I love the sun on my back, the smell of chain oil, the wind in my face…"

Tony and Deirdre spoke in hushed tones through the changing of the nursing shift, blood pressure measurements, and the delivery Deirdre's medicine. Visiting hours were over when Tony said, "I've enjoyed our ride to Rhode Island. And you know what?"

"No, what?"

"Whcn I get you home, I'm going to give you a kiss good night."

"Oh yeah? What kind of a kiss good night?"

"A nice one… a first, but not the last, kiss."

"You can do that now if you like. I had a really good time on our first date."

Chapter 16

The spa

"Ever been to a day spa, Sully?"

"Can't say that I ever have kid. How 'bout you? You ever have cucumber slices on your eyelids? Ever have a deep tissue massage?"

"Yeah, I get a deep tissue massage two or three times a week, but I call it full contact sparring." Sully laughed as they walked up to the front desk. Tony pulled out his badge and said, "Good afternoon, ladies, I'm Detective Capella, and this is Detective Sullivan. Can you tell me where I can find Miss Beth Connors?"

One of the young women behind the counter tapped on her keyboard. "Yes, she's having a manicure. Chandra will show you the way.

An attractive young woman in white stepped from behind the counter. "Follow me, please."

Sully whispered to Tony, "I was hoping for the steam room."

Tony coughed to cover his chuckle.

"Right in here, gentlemen."

Tony was expecting the look of a barbershop but the chairs looked more like overstuffed couches with women getting their finger and toenails painted. Soft music played from hidden speakers. It was like something you would see in old Rome, all that was missing were the grapes. Potted plants lined the walls. Fluted columns formed a circle around a mosaic floor, depicting women in togas picking flowers. Chandra directed them to a pleasantly plump young woman with dark hair in an Egyptian cut, in a loose white bathrobe, her eyes closed, her lips slightly parted, totally relaxed. One girl was painting her toenails, another girl her fingernails. Tony recognized her from the photos in Nancy Miller's bedroom. Tony cleared his throat and asked, "Miss Connors?"

The young woman opened her eyes, and hastily arranged her bathrobe. "Hi, yes. I'm Beth Connors." She looked Tony and Sully over. "You're here to talk about Nancy right? Her dad said you might come and see me."

Sully's eyes narrowed. "Do you talk to Mr. Miller regularly?"

"Well, he is my best friend's dad. We were talking about the funeral, and he told me I might be seeing you."

Tony pulled up a manicurist's stool and sat down. "I know this must be a very hard time for you Miss Connors. Do you know of anyone who would wish Nancy harm?"

"Nancy was a doll. Everyone loved Nancy. Why would anyone want to hurt her?"

"Her father said that she wasn't in a relationship at the time of her death. Is that true?"

Beth took a chocolate covered macadamia nut from a crystal bowl on a dainty table, and popped it into her mouth. "Nancy's very picky. She would take hours just picking out a dress. I tried to set her up a few times, but the guys were never good enough for her. I think she was waiting for a guy like her dad: successful, respectable, wealthy, and handsome... She wouldn't waste her time on a loser."

"Do you know if she had anyone in particular in mind?"

"Not that I know of. She would have told me."

Sully tapped his pencil on his notepad. "Can you tell me where you were at the time of her death?"

"Where I was? I was Nancy's best friend. What? You think I did something to Nancy?" Beth sat up and sent the two salon workers sprawling. "Are you out of your mind!?"

Sully put his palms out and said, "I have to ask Miss Connors, just part of my job... I have to ask."

Looking thoroughly disgruntled, Beth Connors sat back down on the couch. She had quite a different look about her than moments before. She took a few deep breaths to calm herself. "I was in Connecticut visiting my father. We were at his club. Hey, why are you asking all these questions? They said Nancy died from a heart attack. You think somebody killed her? That's crazy."

Tony stood. "Just standard procedure, Miss Connors. We appreciate your time."

Beth waited a few minutes to make sure Tony and Sully were really gone, and picked up her cell phone. "Don? Hey, it's me... Yeah, they just left... Oh, you know, the usual questions... About us? Well, the old one asked if I talk to you regularly. I told him that you're my best friend's dad, which is true, and that we were talking about the funeral... I know, don't worry... Okay. See you soon."

Tony looked down the sites of his pistol and squeezed the trigger 10 times.

"Not bad kid, but watch this..." Sully drew his .45 like a cowboy in the old West and fired six shots. He then pointed his pistol upwards, and opened the cylinder, dropping the spent brass casings to the ground. Before they hit, Sully was grabbing his quick loader and feeding six new rounds in to the empty cylinder. He closed it with a clack, and fired six more rounds in rapid succession, making more holes in his black and white silhouette training target.

"Not bad yourself, Sully. But if you had a 9 mm you could have 10 rounds in a mag. Heck, you could have 20 rounds, they even make them with 30 round mags."

"Yeah, that's just what I need, a 30 round mag. Just in case Poncho Villa shows up with his whole gang." Sully chuckled. "I don't know anyone who's had to fight 10 guys at one time. If I had to, I'd probably call for backup and run like hell. 30 rounds... "Sully was always bashing on Tony's 9 mm.

Tony rolled his eyes and said, "How much does it how cost you when you shoot? Isn't it like, a buck a round? I pay like 25 cents a round for 9 mm."

"Yeah? I don't mind payin' for the extra punch." Sully reloaded, and passed his pistol to Tony. "Here, take a couple of shots with a real gun."

Tony placed his 9 mm on the bench, with the barrel pointing down range, and took Sully's .45. The barrel was longer and the sights were way different. Tony aimed down range at the paper silhouette and hefted the revolver. "Damn, this thing weighs a ton." Tony always preferred shooting two handed, his left palm under his right and left elbow tucked into his chest. Karate helped him with his shooting as well. It made him smooth. The first night he tried skeet shooting, he couldn't miss. It really ticked off the guys who'd been doing it for years. Even when the range master launched a bird when Tony wasn't looking, he still managed to hit it.

Tony lined up the sights and squeezed the trigger, *blam, blam, blam, blam*; Tony's first round hit in the center circle, his second went high, and his third higher still. His fourth round cleared the top of the target. The recoil was worse than Tony had expected. He knew Sully used the maximum grains in his rounds, but *dang*! Tony stopped and fired the last two rounds, emptying the pistol. "This thing's a cannon compared to mine." Tony passed the pistol; grip first, to Sully. "Want to try my 9 mm?"

Sully took back his .45 and emptied the spent shells, "No, that's okay. I gave up cap guns a long time ago."

As Tony and Sully packed up their shooting gear, Sully turned to Tony and said, "I agree with Miss Connors."

"Whatta' ya' mean?"

"She said the thought of someone killing Nancy Miller was crazy, and I agree with her."

"You do?"

Sully shrugged. "Where's the motive? There were no drugs involved. No boyfriend, so it wasn't a crime of passion. Where's the motive?"

Tony asked Sully, "You think it's time to file the report?"

"I think it's past time we closed this case."

As Sully started walking towards the car, Tony said, "Hold up Sully. We can't just close this case."

Sully stopped and asked, "Why not?"

Tony scuffed the ground with his shoe and said, "I don't know… I, I just have a feeling about this."

Sully put his hands on his hips and said, "Is it one of those 'Gee, I've been a detective for a whole week' gut feelings?"

Tony thought, *"Yeah, that's exactly what it is"* but said, "Come on Sully, you told me to swim. Let me swim. Let's go talk to Miller again. I don't know, maybe I missed something that you won't."

It was Sully's turn to roll his eyes. "Okay, kid. Let's go."

"1330 Beacon Street. Here we are, the home of Donald H. Miller." Sully got out of the car and looked up at the brownstone. "What's the H. stand for? Has a lot of money?"

A well-dressed couple on the sidewalk stopped. The man looked at Sully's car with distaste and said, "You can't park that *thing* here. This is reserved parking, for residents only."

Sully didn't even look at the guy. He pulled out his badge, flashed it in the guy's face, and walked past him as if he weren't even there.

Tony thought, *"Maybe I am learning something. I'm going to use that."*

Before Sully rang the buzzer, he turned to Tony and said kindly, "Don't get your hopes up, kid."

Mr. Miller came to the door. "Detectives. I hope you've made some progress."

As they walked into the foyer Tony said, "Well that's just it we –"

Sully cut Tony off. "We've got nothing Mr. Miller. That's why we're here. We've eliminated all the usual suspects, and have come up with nada. Is there anything else you could tell us about your daughter?"

Mr. Miller turned and walked over to the table in the middle of the foyer. He put his hands down on the polished mahogany. "Don't you think I've told you everything?"

Sully walked over to the opposite side of the table. "Think. Was Nancy acting in anyway unusual in the days leading up to her death? Did you have any new visitors?"

"No, Nancy was perfectly fine, and no we didn't have any visitors. We rarely do. I've been reliving those days, minute by minute... No. There's nothing more I can tell you. I wish there were. Did your boys in the lab find anything in Nancy's cosmetics?"

Tony shook his head while Sully tapped his knuckles on the table, deep in thought. "Did anyone besides you and your daughter have a key to your house?"

"Well... just the cleaning company."

Sully looked at Tony, and spoke to Mr. Miller, "And what cleaning company would that be Mr. Miller?"

"The Elite Cleaning Company." Mr. Miller looked at Sully, and a look of comprehension spread over his face. He said, "I'll get you their card."

Chapter 17
Solitaire

Sarah waltzed into Deirdre's room, hopped up on the bed, said brightly, "Hi Deirdre." and gave her a hug. Deirdre hugged back. Sarah looked a little better every day, and her hair was growing back.

Deirdre pulled the playing cards from her game of solitaire into a stack and asked, "How you doing, Sarah?"

Sarah smiled, "Good. The doctors say I'm all done with the skin grafts!"

Deirdre reached out to put her arm around Sarah's shoulders and, at the last moment, thought better of it. Instead she put her fist out for a 'fist bump' and said, "That's great!"

"I won't be able to go out in the sun for a while though."

Deirdre said, "Well, I've got a really cool umbrella at home that you can have. I'll ask my friend, Courtney, to bring it the next time she comes."

"Okay. Who's Courtney?"

"She's my roommate. She has purple hair. You'll like her."

"Purple hair? Like in the cartoons?"

Deirdre smiled and imagined what Courtney would say to that. *She'd probably get a kick out of it.* "Yep, like in the cartoons."

"I want to see that." Sarah pulled two packages of chocolate chip cookies from the pockets of her robe and gave one to Deirdre.

Deirdre took the proffered cookie and asked, "Does that mean you'll be going home soon?"

"Well…" Sarah's shoulders drooped. "I'll be going to live with my grandmother in Chicago."

"Is your grandmother nice?"

"I don't know. I've never met her. Well, I did when I was a baby, but I don't remember her. I saw a picture of her once, in a drawer. She looks nice."

"That's good. I bet you'll make lots of new friends in Chicago."

"I hope so."

"I'm sure you will. A nice girl like you won't have any problems making friends."

Sarah looked imploringly ad Deirdre and asked, "Really?"

"Definitely."

Sarah gave a tiny yawn, searched in vain for another cookie in her pocket, and said, "I'm kinda hungry. I'm going to see if they have any pudding in the cafeteria. Want me to bring you back some?"

"That's ok. I think I'm going to take a little snooze."

Sarah got up on her tip-toes and gave Deirdre a kiss on the forehead, "Ok, good night."

Chapter 18
The Elite Cleaning Company

A rat scurried along the wall of the alley, nose sniffing, whiskers twitching, it's long hairless tail dragging along behind. It stopped and poked its head into an empty chip bag, looking for food. At the sound of footsteps, it sat up on its hind legs and looked about. It didn't run away. It was a city rat, and city rats are braver than most. When the empty soda bottle ricocheted off the wall above its head, it lost what courage it had, and took off, coming to rest under an overloaded dumpster.

Tony looked to Sully, who had just thrown the plastic bottle, and said, "Hey, what did that rat ever do to you?"

Sully said, disgusted, "I hate rats. They eat holes in walls, and poop all over the place. It's nasty." Sully felt Tony's lingering gaze and said, "I wasn't tryin' to kill it, okay? Just scare the little furball. Jeez, why don't you adopt one or somethin'?"

Tony chuckled as he and Sully walked down the alley. They took a right hand turn and walked down a *smaller* alley. The red brick buildings were so close together that it seemed more like dusk than mid-day.

One thing Tony liked about alleys in Boston was that they never changed. People spent the money on renovating the front of the buildings, and never a dime for the backs. The alleys in Boston look the same as when they were first built. Wrought iron grates cover the lower windows, and wrought iron flower boxes, bereft of flowers, still hang beneath the higher windows. Many of the alleys, like the one they were in now, were cobblestoned. Tony thought, *"It wouldn't be surprising to see a horse drawn carriage come around the corner."* The smell of the alley quickly drove such romantic thoughts from Tony's mind. It smelled like a mixture of urine, stale beer and garbage.

They passed one door after another, and finally came

upon a faded rusty sign. It was only just legible and read "Elite Cleaning Company". Sully laughed, "Elite Cleaning. Ha!"

When Tony went to knock, Sully stopped him, and said softly, "If you knock, they might just lock the door. Play it cool inside. If these cleaners are illegal immigrants, and we spook them, they'll disappear" Sully snapped his fingers "like that!"

Sully then turned the knob, opened the door and stepped through. Old tin lights hung from the ceiling, with what had to be 25 Watt incandescent bulbs, half of which were working. The short hall led straight to a flight of stairs done in what must once have been a nice carpet. Now it was covered in filth. Graffiti covered the crumbling plaster walls. Sully trudged up the stairs followed by Tony. When they reached the second floor, directly across from the staircase, was a glass door with "office" painted on it. The glass was cracked and taped. Sully turned the knob and walked through.

Behind the desk was a very overweight dark skinned woman, with poorly dyed red hair. In the corner was a car seat with a baby in it, fast asleep. The woman looked up from her meal of microwave mac and cheese, and was startled to see two men standing before her. She screamed, "Ieeeee! Deus me proteja! (God protect me!)" Which woke the baby, who also started to scream. The woman looked at the baby, and shot Tony and Sully a dirty look as if to say, *"See what you've done!"* With difficulty, the woman stood, walked across the room and picked up the baby seat. She brought it back, put it on her desk, sat with a thump, and made cooing sounds to quiet the child.

Sully sighed. "Você fala Inglês?" he asked the woman in Portuguese.

"Si. Yes, I speak English. What do you want?"

"Boston police ma'am. We need a list of the cleaners you send to 1330 Beacon Street, the home of Mr. Donald Miller."

The woman's eyes grew large, "Why? What happened? Did someone steal something?"

"We just need to ask them a few questions, strictly routine. Nothing to worry about."

She opened a drawer in the desk, "Um minuto. Give me a minute." and pulled out a manila folder. "Lucinda and Rosaria Tavares. They're sisters. They always work together."

Sully pulled out his notepad, "Do you have their address?"

"Si."

Sully jotted it down, and Tony made a mental note to pick up a notepad for himself.

Sully closed his pad and said, "Muito obrigado, Senhora. I'll let you get back to your lunch."

As Tony and Sully turned to leave she said, "Um minuto…" and looked at the file again. She looked up at Sully and said, "They are on a job right now… The Independent Motel, working from 8:00 to 7:00"

When they got back to the car, Sully made for the trunk instead of the driver seat. He popped the lid, reached in and pulled out a green trash bag. After rifling through it for a minute, he tossed Tony an old gray sweatshirt from a community college, and pulled one out for himself.

Tony asked, "What's this for?"

Sully put an arm through his sweatshirt, "We can't go down to that motel wearing suits. We'd stick out like a sore thumb. In the old days, when all cops wore uniforms, word would travel through a neighborhood so fast, that all the scum and riffraff would disappear like magic."

Tony took off his suit jacket and tie, and slipped the sweatshirt over his head. It was several sizes too big and looked ridiculous, as if he were wearing a circus tent. He pushed the sleeves up to his elbows so that he could at least use his hands. Sully looked him up and down, "Mess up your hair. You look too… clean."

They got in Sully's car and headed for the motel. The closer they got, the more Tony could see what Sully was talking about. The neighborhood had a feel of seediness and neglect. The road was full of potholes, and weeds were growing from the cracks in the sidewalk. Little piles of tempered glass sparkled in the sun; remnants of car windows that had been smashed. Burglar grates and plywood covered the windows of the houses.

As they pulled into the motel parking lot, they passed a group of hookers standing on the corner. As Tony and Sully got out of the car, two of the prostitutes walked over, "Hey, you want a good time?"

The weather was warm so they were each wearing halter-tops, short skirts and high heels. Sully reached into his wallet.

Tony was surprised when, instead of pulling out his badge, he pulled out two business cards. "You girls are kinda' young to be on the street." He handed each of the girls a card, "This guys a friend of mine. He runs a shelter over on Washington Street. Get yourself over there, and he'll help you out." The girls looked to be about 16 or 17 years old. "He's helped out a lot of girls: food, clothes, and gotten a lot of them into school. Check it out. You girls are friends right? Well, do each other a solid and get over there. This guy's mad chill."

The girls took the cards and walked away. Tony cocked an eyebrow and asked, "Mad chill?"

Sully grinned, "Yeah, you gotta' talk the talk with these youngsters."

Tony and Sully walked toward the front of the motel. Tony stopped and said, "I think I saw this motel in a zombie movie… No, that one was nicer."

They passed a swimming pool, empty, but for the 5 or 6 inches of rust colored water in the bottom.

Sully turned to Tony and said, "Remind me to send some blues over here to make sure they chain off that pool before someone breaks their neck some night."

They walked inside and Sully motioned Tony to the front desk. Tony pulled out his badge before the attendant could ask him if he wanted a room. "Detectives Capella and Sullivan. We need to see a couple of your cleaners. Lucinda and Rosaria Tavares."

The attendant looked pretty seedy. He was gulag thin, pale, and had gray hair with bald patches. It looked like he was either on heroin or had come off heroin in the not too distant past. He sported two large earrings, tattooed sleeves and a gray ponytail.

The attendant asked, "What did they do?"

Tony put his hand on the counter, and then thinking better of it, wiped his hand on his pants, "We just want to ask them a few questions. Now, if you could tell me where they are…"

"Yeah, they're cleaning the third floor today."

There was no elevator, so Tony and Sully walked up the stairs to the third floor. The motel was done in a 1970's style, probably because it was built in the 70's, and had hadn't been remodeled since. As they walked along the hall, which smelled strongly of marijuana, they came to a cleaning cart stacked with towels, sheets and cleaning supplies. The motel room door was open, with a "House Cleaning" hanger hung on the doorknob.

Tony walked in first and called out, "Hello? Rosaria, Lucinda?"

A voice answered from the bathroom, "Hello, yes?"

Two women met Tony and Sully at the door. Tony showed his badge. "I'm detective Cappella, and this is Detective Sullivan."

The two women were obviously sisters. They each wore a matching gray dress and white apron, both were petite, and had dark hair and dark eyes. They looked to be about 35, but were probably younger. Tony thought, *"No, they're probably closer to 25. Years of hard work has probably aged them prematurely."* He asked them politely, "Would you like to sit down?" He motioned toward the bed. "We'd just like to ask you a few questions."

The sisters looked at each other apprehensively, and sat down on the freshly made bed. They held each other's hands, like little girls do when they expect to be scolded. As the women looked so nervous, Tony spoke softly, "I understand that you clean Mr. Miller's house on Beacon Street. Is that right?"

One of the women, either Rosaria or Lucinda, he couldn't tell which, said, "Yes, sir. Did we do something wrong?"

As Tony opened his mouth to speak, the other sister said, "I knew it. I knew I would get caught. I can't believe this. I'm going to get fired." She broke down sobbing. Her sister put her arm around her shoulders and started speaking in Portuguese.

Tony gave it a moment for the sobs to slow down and said, "It's okay. It's okay. Just tell me what happened."

When the woman looked up and saw the compassion in Tony's face, she said haltingly, "It was an accident. I dropped my bucket. And it just broke. It just broke."

Tony nodded encouragingly and said, "Go on."

"I dropped the bucket in the bathroom and the tile just broke. It was all cracked. And I, I didn't want to get fired."

Tony looked to Sully who said, "Okay, so the tile broke. What did you do next?"

"I called my cousin, Hernando, and he said he knew a guy. So I told him where I was. A few hours later, this guy comes to the house. He had tools and everything, and I said, 'you have to fix this before Mr. Miller gets home.' So he went into the bathroom and he fix the tile. He broke out the old one, and glued in a new one. Then he put that stuff around it, argamassa. What's that stuff called?" she asked her sister.

"Grout."

"Yes, grout."

Tony waited for the woman to finish talking, but it seemed she had. He asked, "Do you know this guy's name?"

The woman looked to her sister who nodded as if to say, *"Go ahead and tell him."*

"Henrique Parreira."

Sully wrote the name down and asked, "Do you know where Mr. Parreira lives?"

The woman nodded and said, "Fall River."

When Tony and Sully got back to the station parking lot, Tony changed out of Sully's old sweatshirt and back into his jacket and tie. "Gee, I wish I had a picture of myself in this get-up. My mom would get a kick out of it."

As Tony walked toward the front steps of the station, he looked up and saw one of the many video cameras looking down at him. As they walked in the front doors Tony said, "Hey Sully, you go on up, I gotta' talk to somebody."

Sully nodded and headed upstairs to his desk. Tony headed down. He knocked on the door of the IT department and walked in. He looked around the room and didn't see anyone. "Hey, Sean you in here?"

A head popped up from behind a control panel. "Hey Tony, what can I do for you? Not the password again?"

"No. But I really need your help. If I email you a picture of a young woman who got to work at 9 o'clock in the morning in the Financial District, could you back-track her from video camera footage from the neighborhood? I want to know if she stopped in anywhere, or talked to any strangers on the way to work."

Sean smiled. "That's the kind of work I like the best. Yeah, absolutely, I can do that. We're talking about your Nancy Miller case right? I've checked out her computer: email, social media, nothing unusual. Give me as much info as you can, you know, if she took the bus, the T, a cab or whatever, whatever you can give me."

"That's awesome. I'll go upstairs and email you everything right now. Thanks, Sean."

Tony took the steps back up to his desk two at a time.

When he got there he emailed Sean everything he had on Nancy Miller.

Sully looked over at Tony typing away on his computer and said, "Someone's a busy little beaver. What are you up to?"

Tony smiled. "Modern technology, Sully. Modern technology."

Sully stood up. "Hey it's getting late and I want to go home. Let's check in with the Captain and tell him we're going to Fall River in the morning."

Tony hit send, shut down his computer and followed Sully into the Captains office.

Capt. Gonzalez looked tired. He yawned and said, "Yeah, no sweat. I'll give 'em a call at the station down in Fall River and set things up. I'll make sure they loan you a cop who speaks the lingo. Don't be surprised if it doesn't lead to anything. I still think the Miller case is 'death by natural causes'." The captain picked up the phone. As he dialed he said, "Complete waste of resources, but Miller's a friend of the Mayor..."

The two detectives walked across the parking lot and stopped at Sully's car. As Sully unlocked his car door, Tony said, "I didn't know you spoke Spanish, Sully."

"Portuguese, Tony. You know, it took me the longest time to figure out that Portuguese isn't Spanish. I mean, Portuguese is a language all on its own. I speak a little Spanish, but years ago I'd be talking away and no one could understand me, then I find out they're speaking another language. You learn something new every day."

"So how did you learn to speak Portuguese?"

"There's an old Portuguese man two doors down from me. Gave me lessons."

"Wow, Sully. I'm impressed."

"Yeah, that's me. I'm impressive. G' night, kid."

"Night, Sully."

Tony was tired, as he walked to his Jeep, he debated whether he should go home and take a shower, or just drive over to say a quick "hi" to Deirdre. He opted for the latter.

Chapter 19
Nose to nose

Tony fidgeted in the hospital elevator. He asked himself, *"Should I visit tonight? Is it too much, too soon?"*

He pushed his doubts aside and stopped in the men's room to splash some water on his face before going to Deirdre's room. Her door was ajar and the lights were dim. He tapped lightly on the doorjamb. Deirdre answered with a soft, "Hello?"

Tony poked his head inside and said, "Hey."

Deirdre was reading with the help of a small clip on book lamp.

She put her book down on the over-bed table. "Hey, back at you."

Tony felt a little uncomfortable. It was the "day after the first date" and he wasn't exactly sure how to play it, but when he saw Deirdre's welcoming smile he didn't hesitate to lean down and give her a kiss. It was the most natural thing in the world. He stood up and started to reach for a chair, but Deirdre caught his arm, and patted the side of the hospital bed. "Hey, sit here."

Tony sat. Deirdre studied his face. "You look tired, long day?"

Tony nodded, "Yeah, pretty long; a lot of running around." He took off his suit jacket and tossed it on the chair, followed by his tie. He looked self-conscious and said, "I'm not sure you want me to sit too close. I came over right from work. I hope I don't... I hope I don't smell too bad."

Deirdre sat up and smelled his chest, "No, you smell fine."

Tony sat down on the edge of the bed. He reached down with his right hand and ran his fingers through her hair. "I like your hair."

Deirdre reached up with her right hand and put it on his

cheek, hooked her hand around his neck, and pulled him down for a kiss. When people kiss, a time comes when they mutually stop kissing. This was not one of those times.

It started like a light rain, a summer rain; welcome after the heat of the day. As they kissed, Tony felt the warmth of Deirdre's body against his chest. He didn't know how they had come to be that close, it just sort of happened. He was aware of Deirdre's breath on his face. His heart thumped, he could feel it beating, or maybe that was Deirdre's heart? Each breath of air filled his lungs as if he had never breathed before.

As they kissed, Deirdre felt a shadow fall over them, but it felt like something happening very far away. She was completely lost in their embrace. Two people coming together in the dark, once alone, once bound by the chains of insecurity, chains which they helped each other to break, there in a darkened hospital room, with the simple act of a kiss... and it was so easy, as if they were simply brushing the sand off each other's shoulders after a day on the beach... "*I love the way you smell. I love the way you taste*," she thought. It was as if she had never kissed before... time slipped by...

Again the shadow fell over them. Again she was lost in the kiss. She had no idea how long it went on. She had no concept of time. She knew only that she didn't want it to end. ... It wasn't sexual... It was *beyond* sexual.

Tony's heart beat faster, the kiss that had started as a light rain was turning into a tropical storm, heavy droplets washed over his face and chest... he took Deirdre's lower lip between his teeth... his hand moved down the curve of her back, he could feel her respond... Deirdre's fingers closed about a handful of Tony's hair, she pulled him in harder... Once again the shadow fell over them, like a cloud passing over the moon, but this time it didn't move on. "Hmmmm." Tony and Deirdre opened their eyes at the same time and just stared at each other, nose to nose... as they moved to kiss once again, they were interrupted by a second, louder and longer, "Hmmmmm."

Deirdre and Tony slowly looked towards the door. In the doorway stood a nurse, her hands on her hips. "Do you know what time it is? It's 2 o'clock in the morning! I walked past three times and I didn't want to interrupt, but it's 2:00 in the morning! Sir, you are going to have to let my patient sleep."

Tony didn't move. He just sat there holding Deirdre's hand. The nurse stamped her foot and pointed out the door, "Sir, I am going to have to ask you to leave!"

Tony looked up at the nurse, smiled and said, "Okay nurse, I'll go. Just let me give Deirdre a kiss good night."

Chapter 20
Fall River

Tony and Sully were in the fast lane doing 75, Southbound on Route 24 towards Fall River. Sully was in the driver seat. "You look like crap."

Tony turned bloodshot eyes to Sully. "Thanks a lot, Sull. I didn't really sleep last night." He gazed out the window and watched the treetops zip by against the early morning sky; the branches an ever-changing stained glass.

Sully passed a group of cars. "Did you try warm milk?"

Tony chuckled. "No. Maybe next time."

"Up late talking to the Irish girl?"

"Yeah."

"You like this girl, huh?"

"Yeah... I do." Tony's eyes shifted to a group of seagulls, flying in lazy circles over a landfill. "It's weird. I've dated a lot of girls, but-."

Sully chuckled and said, "The understatement of the year."

"Come on, Sull. It hasn't been that many."

"Not from what your mother tells me."

"Is that what mom says?"

"Yeah, and they usually lasts a week. Two at most."

Tony shrugged and said, "That sounds about right."

"So what's different about this one?"

I don't know. It's weird. She makes me feel like... Like I'm 16 years old again."

"That's a scary thought!"

"Nah, it's a good thing." Sully shook his head and said, "You're scaring me, Tony. I'll have to run a background check on this girl. McDonough, right?"

Tony turned his head to face Sully, smiled and said, "Yeah, Sull. I'm sure she's on the FBI's most wanted list."

"Now I'm definitely going to run a background check."

Tony yawned and stretched.

Sully said, "We got an hour and a half before we get there. Why don't you kick back and catch some Z's."

Tony stretched out as best he could and said, "Sounds like a plan."

It felt like Tony had just closed his eyes when he was awakened by the slamming of the back door. He stretched and looked over his left shoulder. A female cop dressed in the livery of the Fall River Police Department sat in the back seat. "Good morning," she said with exaggerated cheeriness. "Sorry to wake you up."

Sully got into the driver's seat. Tony turned to Sully, and said through clenched teeth, "Thanks a lot, Sully. You couldn't have woken me up?"

Sully smiled at the female police officer, as if they were sharing a very funny private joke. The female cop smiled back at Sully, thumped Tony on the shoulder, and said in the voice of one talking to a baby. "He probably didn't want to wake you up. You looked so cute there in nappy time."

Tony pulled the seatbelt down from where it had been digging into to his neck. "Ha ha, very funny."

She laughed. "Take it easy kid, we're just yanking your chain. I'm Luci Avilla."

Though a decade younger than Sully, Tony could see that they were kindred spirits. Sgt. Avilla shook Tony's hand. "So, you're looking for Henrique Parreira? I checked the database and there's no wants or warrants. He's probably new to the country. What do you guys want him for?"

Tony let Sully do the talking, seeing as these two were getting along so well. Sully looked over his shoulder as he was pulling out of the parking lot. "For questioning in the death of a young woman."

Avilla nodded. "What can you tell me about this Parreira?"

"Not much, he did some tile work in Boston on the 17th."

"That isn't much. It's lucky you guys got me. I grew up in Fall River. I have family in construction. If they don't know this guy, they'll know who will. He's probably an illegal, and the illegals stick together. Most of them don't speak any English, so when they need work, they have to go to one of the bosses."

Sully looked in the rearview mirror at Sergeant Avilla and asked, "One of the bosses?"

"Yeah, the guys that have been here for a while sometimes set themselves up as contractors, and either hire, or subcontract jobs out to the illegals. They speak English, they get most of the money, and do hardly any of the work. In exchange they transport people to and from jobs, pay them under the table, and get them fake IDs."

Tony made a sour face. "Sounds like quite a racket. Sounds like they're totally taking advantage of them."

"Some do. But most take good care of their illegals. They have to, or the money'll dry up. Some of the bad bosses have been found floating face down in the bay, but the good ones'll get their workers what they can't get here: medical attention, affordable and illegal housing. They'll even get their kids into school under fake names."

"Will they cooperate with the police?"

Sgt. Avilla smiled. "They'll cooperate with me. I'm one of them."

She took out her cell phone and started speaking in Portuguese at what sounded like a million miles an hour. When she hung up she said, "It's probably only one or two bosses that would handle that area. They each have their own territories."

Tony looked over his shoulder. "It sounds like the Mafia."

"The Mafia without the drugs and the prostitution. These are construction bosses we're going to see. There are bosses that handle prostitution, but the others won't have anything to do with them. They're treated like the scum they are, considered the lowest of the low. They give the other bosses a bad name, the illegals too."

Sergeant Avilla directed Sully up a winding city street of triple-deckers. "Okay, the brown one on the corner."

In front of the brown triple-decker were parked several trucks and vans with ladders on top, or wheelbarrows in the back. As Sully parked the car, Sgt. Avilla said, "Let me do all the talking." She turned to Tony and said, "You wait here. I think three of us'll scare 'em."

Sgt. Avilla and Sully got out of the car and disappeared into the triple-decker.

While Tony waited, he pulled out his phone and dialed Deirdre, "Hey Deirdre, it's Tony... Yeah, it's good to hear your voice, too. I'm workin' a case down here in beautiful Fall River, Massachusetts, and I thought I'd give ya' a call and say hey, and, you know, that last night was awesome... Did that nurse give you a hard time after I left? ... That's good...Yeah I'd like t' do it again, too. The sooner the better..."

Ten minutes later Sully and Avilla were walking back to the car. Tony said a hurried goodbye before Sgt. Avilla hopped in the back seat and said, "We're in luck. Parreira's working on a construction job today and it's only 20 minutes away."

As they drove over a long iron bridge, Tony got a text from Sean: **TONY, BACKTRACKED MILLER WITH VIDEO FOOTAGE FROM WHITNEY AND BROWN TO COFFEE SHOP. SHE STAYED 20 MINUTES. EXAMINING FOOTAGE. WILL LET YOU KNOW. P.S. SHE'S HOT!** Tony shook his head and thought, *"She's hot? Really, Sean?"*

The smell of salt water was pleasantly strong. Tony looked out the window at the steel grey ocean peeking through between the huge cylindrical natural gas tanks they drove by. The salt air seemed to jog Sully's memory, who turned to Sergeant Avilla and asked, "Hey, is there a fish market around here? I told my wife I was going to Fall River, and she told me to pick up some fish."

Tony made a sour face. "Sully, you really want to drive around all day with a fish? I mean, won't it get pretty rank?"

Sully took a turn and said, "All day? Come on, this should take about 15 minutes tops. Fall River's famous for fish."

They pulled up to a large construction site surrounded by a high chain link fence. Workers were unloading and setting up concrete forms; long sheets of plywood with steel brackets to connect them together. Sergeant Avilla didn't object to Tony coming this time, so the three exited the car, and walked over to the construction site. They headed straight for the oldest man on the job site. He looked to be about 50, was well muscled and seemed to be directing things from atop a pallet of cinder blocks.

Sergeant Avilla approached him and questioned him in Portuguese, he replied, "Parreira? Ele está lá." and pointed to a shirtless young man in his late teens or early 20s.

Heads started to turn towards the uniformed Sgt. Avilla and the suited Tony and Sully. When Parreira saw the trio looking directly at him, he dropped his plywood and took off like a shot. Sully slapped Tony on the back and said, "Go get 'im, tiger."

Tony hit the ground running. Parreira flew past his coworkers as Tony gave chase through the construction site. They wove in and out of workers and over stacks of lumber. "*He's fast*," thought Tony.

As he closed the distance, one of the construction workers dropped his shovel front of Tony's legs. The shovel's handle caught a stake in the ground and Tony went down hard. Tony grabbed his shin, which felt as if someone had struck it with a hammer, and looked up at the worker who'd dropped the shovel. The construction worker looked down at Tony and said with a look of concern, "Senhor? desculpe."

Tony didn't speak Portuguese, but he knew what the worker meant, and didn't believe it for a second. Tony got to his feet quickly and continued the pursuit. He rounded an office trailer and stopped to look to his left and right. There was no sign of Parreira. He backtracked, looking as he went. He checked the construction trailer, and behind several stacks of construction supplics. Several minutes later he was back with Sully and Sergeant Avilla. Tony breathed in deeply and said, "I lost him."

Sgt. Avilla turned back to the car. "I'll call in an A.P.B."

Chapter 21
Girl Talk

Deirdre sat propped up on innumerable pillows as Courtney, the tip of her tongue between her teeth in concentration, painted Deirdre's fingernails a garish pink. Deirdre shook her head and said, "Bright pink Court?"

"He'll love it, Dee. Trust me. Just leave this to the professional. You think you'll see him tonight?"

Deirdre looked at the vase of flowers on the window-sill, a gift from Tony, and said, "I don't know. He's down in Fall River on a case."

"What kind of a case?"

"I don't know. He hasn't really told me anything about his work; just that he made detective."

"He's pretty young to be a detective." Courtney followed her gaze and asked, "More flowers? He is so into you Dee."

Deirdre smiled and blushed.

Courtney, finished with Deirdre's right hand, started painting the nails on her left. She asked, "How's the back?"

"About a zillion times better." Deirdre rolled her shoulders. "I can't wait to this rod out of my leg. Twice a night I go to turn in my sleep, and the pain wakes me up."

"I can't imagine."

"How are things in the salon?"

"Busy. Tara's thinking of leaving and setting up a shop of her own. She asked me to come with her."

"Isn't that mad-expensive?"

"It is, but her parents have money."

"Would you do it?"

"I don't know. Could you see me as a business owner? I love cutting hair, and I do ok now. I'm not sure I see myself doing paperwork every night. I see what the owner has to go through."

"Is it a lot?"

"Yeah, she's a real stress monkey. You'd think that with a busy salon, she'd be swimming in money, but some months I think she just breaks even."

"Seriously?"

"Everything adds up: Rent, utilities, insurance…"

"So, do you think you'll do it, I mean, if Tara starts a new salon?"

"I don't know, Dee. I think I'm too young. There's still so much a lot I'd like to do."

"Like what?"

"Like have some fun, travel… See the world."

"You gonna go on a cruise court?"

"Not likely. I'd like to do the whole backstreet thing, you know, visit the little villages that time forgot. One of my uncles used to travel to Europe. When he was in Budapest he saw a little town in a magazine that looked really cool, so he and his buddies decided to go. They got on the train, and six hours later they got to this little town in Eastern Europe. When they got there they found the place almost deserted and the people they did see weren't friendly at all. It turns out that there were two towns with the same name in different countries, and my uncle had the wrong country."

"That stinks."

"You'd think so, but my uncle and his buddies had a great time in the town that time forgot. It's like one of those islands that are so remote that nothing changes over time; like the Galapagos"

"Well, you're going to have to take me with you. I don't know if I want my best friend traveling all over Europe by herself."

"Who says I'm going by myself? Maybe I'll find myself a hot cop to take me."

"Want me to ask Tony if he has a friend?"

Courtney laughed and said, "Nah, I don't like cops."

Deirdre punched her in lightly the arm and said, "Court!"

"Kidding, Dee."

Chapter 22
Someone who runs.

Someone who runs is usually guilty, and Henrique was running. When Henrique heard the policeman's footsteps fade, he crawled out of the ditch in which he was hiding. Quickly and quietly he ran for the chain-link fence that surrounded the construction site.

Henrique worked hard every day, and was in great shape. He scaled the ten-foot fence with ease and landed lightly on the other side. He was no stranger to running. He'd run from the INS, and from the police in Brazil. When he thought about it, it seemed he'd been running most of his life.

Henrique knew he had to move. He knew he only had a few minutes before the neighborhood would be swarming with police. He took his tank top out of his back pocket, slipped it on, and started walking down the sidewalk towards his apartment. He stopped suddenly, and said, "Eu não posso ir para o meu apartamento. Esse é o primeiro lugar que eles vão olhar. (I can't go to my apartment. That's the first place they'll look.)" He could go to his Aunt Rosa's house. She would hide him there, but she lived in New Bedford. He'd taken the bus to New Bedford once or twice, so he turned down a side street, avoiding the main thoroughfare and made his way towards the bus stop. He put his head down and his hands in his pockets, trying to remain as inconspicuous as possible. As he was passing an old man washing his car in his driveway, the old man narrowed his eyes, and looked at him suspiciously. "*I must look nervous.*" Henrique thought. Another block down he passed a group of girls texting on their cell phones and got an idea. He put his cupped his hand to his cheek, pretending to have a cell phone, and chatted away as if he were talking to one of his friends in Brazil. 15 minutes later he came out on the main drag near the bus stop. As he came out of the side street, he stopped and looked to make sure there were no police cars before making his way to the stop.

There was a group waiting for the bus: an old man with a cane, a young woman with a baby stroller, a middle-aged woman with plastic grocery bags on her arms, and half a dozen teenagers. Henrique walked over and stood with the teenagers, trying to blend in with them. He tried not to fidget while he waited. It was hard. He heard the rumble of the bus and looked to his left in time to see the bus driving past in a cloud of diesel exhaust. "What happened, why did it not stop?"

The old woman turned and said, "Está cheio (It's full)."

Henrique's heart beat loudly in his chest. He knew he couldn't wait on the street for the next bus. As the teenagers walked away, Henrique walked behind them, trying to appear as one of the group, and at the same time, trying not to frighten them. The group of teenagers turned from the sidewalk and walked towards a convenience store. Not knowing what else to do, Henrique followed in their wake. As they neared the store, a red four-door Corolla pulled up and parked near the entrance. A woman hopped out of the car and ran inside.

The car was still running... Acting in desperation, Henrique jumped into the car and put it in reverse. Horns honked as he flew backwards into the busy thoroughfare. Henrique crossed himself and hit the gas. "Oh meu Deus, oh meu Deus, o que eu fiz? (Oh my God, oh my God, what did I do?)"

When he came to a red light he stopped and wiped the sweat from his brow. He looked in the rearview mirror, thinking that the police must be right behind him. There were no police, but when he looked down he saw, to his horror, a little blonde girl strapped in a car seat.

The light turned green. Henrique stared into the rearview mirror, and the little girl stared back. He was prompted into action by the car beeping behind him and the driver gesturing wildly. Henrique looked forward and hit the gas. If he could make it to his Aunt Rosa's house, he'd be okay. Henrique had only driven a few times in his life. His knuckles were white on the steering wheel, and sweat poured down his face. Pop music played on the radio, but he didn't dare take his eyes off the road to turn it off. He could hear sirens in the distance, and the little girl stirring in the back seat. Henrique drove up the on-ramp, onto Route 195 towards New Bedford, and got into the fast lane.

A policeman driving in the opposite direction looked him right in the eye and turned on his flashing lights. Henrique sped up. Jersey barriers separated the east and west bound lanes, so it took a few minutes for the police car to catch up. The little girl in the backseat started to cry, and from what Henrique could understand was calling for her mother. Henrique said, "Fique quieto, fique quieto. (Be quiet, be quiet.)"

The little girl's calls for help were making Henrique even more nervous. When he looked again in his rearview mirror, there was not one, but three police cars behind him. They were staying about ten car lengths behind, probably because of the little girl in the car.

When Henrique looked at the next highway road sign, he realized that while he had been looking back at the police, he had missed the exit to New Bedford. He brought his fist down hard on the steering wheel. As he drove, he wondered where the highway would lead, not knowing that only miles ahead lay the Atlantic Ocean.

The closer Henrique got to Cape Cod, the marshier his surroundings became. The buildings off the highway became scarcer, until there was only marshy woods and scrubland. It was quite different from his tropical Brazilian homeland and, to Henrique, it looked ugly and desolate. He thought of what would happen if he were caught. Would they send him back to Brazil? Or would he go to prison in the United States for all the laws he was breaking now?

Kidnapping had to be serious he thought, probably just under murder.

As he looked to his right, several more police cars were pulling onto the highway. One Mustang black-and-white zipped by, pulled up in front of him, and started to slow down. As Henrique moved to the next lane, the police car followed his movements and blocked him. In anger and frustration, Henrique hit the gas and tapped the back of the police car. Not wanting any harm to come to the little girl, the officer pulled over and let Henrique by. As Henrique passed the Mustang, he looked with fear at the policeman, and saw only a look of determination in return. He wondered why the police let him go by, and understood in the next moment. A mile ahead of him was a solid line of police cars with flashing lights across the whole width of the eastbound highway.

Henrique hit the brakes, threw the car in park, opened the door and vaulted over the Jersey barriers. Cars beeped, skidded, and swerved as Henrique made his way across the westbound lanes of the highway. He jumped the guardrail and made his way into the marshy woods.

He could hear his mother's voice inside his head, "Corra, Henrique, corra! (Run, Henrique, run!)"

His feet squashed on the wet ground as he made for the trees. As the trees became larger, the ground became firmer, and the thickets became thicker. Thorns scratched at his arms and legs as he ran. His foot caught a root and he went down, scraping his forearms. He didn't know where he was going, but he knew he had to keep running. He hoped that crossing the highway would buy him enough time to get away. After running for 15 or 20 minutes, the trees and shrubs started to thin. As he broke from the woods he stopped short. In front of him spread marshy grassland as far as the eye could see. He turned and made his way back into the woods. Once again under the trees, Henrique stopped to catch his breath. He decided to run west instead of east, since the police knew he wanted to go east. He changed his all out run to a steady jog.

The trees formed a peninsula in a sea of grass, and Henrique stood at the tip. He could see buildings and a gas station in the distance. Dusk was falling and he felt his best chance was to wait for nightfall to cross the open ground. He crawled into a group of bushes and waited.

As he waited, he pulled thorns from his arms and legs, and thought back to his life in Brazil. To say that he had been poor would be an understatement. He, his mother, brothers and sisters had lived in a small shack on the side of the mountain near the emerald mines. That's where all the trouble had started. At 15, Henrique had started to work in the mine carrying dirt out and water in for the miners. One day, as he was hauling buckets, he walked past the weighing station. When he thought no one was looking he grabbed a handful of the rough stones. He could have fed his poor family for a year with the money they brought in. When he got home that night and showed them to his mother she had started to cry, "Henrique, o que você fez (Henrique, what have you done?)"

Then the men came. They heard them coming, cursing and kicking in doors. Henrique's mother took him by the shoulders and told him, "Corra, Henrique, corra! (Run, Henrique, run!)" and run he did.

He ran through the village, and just when he thought he was in the clear, a man grabbed him by the scruff of the neck and hissed, "Venha aqui seu pequeno rato de sarjeta. (Come here, you little gutter rat.)"

In the struggle Henrique picked up a stick, and jabbed it into the man's face. The man had lost his eye. Henrique hadn't stopped running since.

At the next village he got on the bus for the capital, and met up with other Brazilians on their way to the United States. A woman who had lost her son took pity on him and brought him along.

As dusk deepened, Henrique heard a low thrumming sound in the distance. As it got louder, he felt the hairs on the back of his neck stand up. "Um helicóptero. (A helicopter.)" he thought.

He peered out from his nest of bushes and saw a searchlight, bright as day, slicing back and forth across the canopy of the woods. He crouched down as it passed overhead kicking up leaves and dust. He breathed a sigh of relief as the sound faded, only to be replaced minutes later by the sound of dogs. He could wait no longer. He crawled out from the bushes and started running as fast as he could towards the buildings in the distance. As he ran the ground became wetter and wetter, and soon he was struggling. He crawled on his hands and knees, grabbing bunches of grass and pulling himself forward. Mud streaked his face and body. The stench of rotting vegetation pierced his nostrils. He wanted to be sick. As he reached the shore of the sea of grass, he stood and staggered slowly forward. When the spotlight hit him in the face, blinding him, he knew it was over. He put his hands up and fell down on his knees, utterly exhausted.

Henrique sat in the interrogation room, handcuffed to a desk. Tony, Sully and Sergeant Avilla sat opposite him. Henrique told his story in a listless monotone. He was defeated, broken. After Henrique had explained why he had run, that he had stabbed the man in the face causing him to lose an eye, Sully said, "Sgt. Avilla, my Portuguese isn't as good as I would like, and I wouldn't want there to be any misunderstanding. Would you tell Henrique that he's wanted in Brazil? Tell him that if he cooperates we can ship him back there. He was 15 when it happened, so he'd be tried as a juvenile. He'll probably get off since it was self-defense, and if he is found guilty he'll only do 1 to 3 years, tops. Tell him if he doesn't cooperate, we can keep him here, where he'll go to prison and do 25 to life for kidnapping someone under 14."

Sgt. Avilla rattled away in Portuguese. She turned to Sully and said, "He says he *is* cooperating. He says that he knows nothing of Nancy Miller."

Sully looked Henrique in the eye, "Tell him I don't believe him."

Henrique and Sgt. Avilla spoke back and forth. Sgt. Avilla said, "He asks where Nancy Miller Died."

Henrique spoke again and the Sgt. Translated, "He asks when Nancy Miller died."

When Sgt. Avilla told Henrique he replied, "Quando ela morreu, eu estava, eu estava aqui, em uma cela. (When she died, I was I was here, in a cell.)"

Sully frowned and asked, "Here? In the Police Station?"

Sgt. Avilla translated. She and Henrique talked back and forth before the Sergeant said, "It seems that he had had an argument with his neighbors about their chickens waking him up in the morning. He was arrested for disorderly conduct and released the following day."

Further questioning revealed that Henrique had indeed been in a cell at the time of Nancy Miller's death. The Fall River police corroborated his story when they pulled up his mug shot and the time of his arrest.

Sully sighed and shook his head, "Well, I guess that clears Henrique Parreira." A smile spread over his face.

Tony looked askance at Sully and asked, "What are you smiling at? We're back to square one."

"Chickens... I bet Henrique's pretty glad his neighbors have chickens now."

Tony looked to Sergeant Avilla and asked, "What do you think? Will they send him back to Brazil, or will he go to prison for kidnapping?"

Sgt. Avilla looked at Tony and said, "They'll send him back if I have anything to do with it. Like I said, I'm one of them."

Tony was glad to hear it. He felt for this teenager behind the desk.

Sully yawned and said, "Looks like it's time to go

home, Tony… and it looks like it's time to tell the Captain we're closing this case…"

Sgt. Avilla asked Sully, "Aren't you forgetting something?"

"What?"

"Your fish."

Henrique watched their conversation uncomprehendingly. When they were finished talking, Sgt Avilla told him that she would do what she could for him. When she was finished he said, "Por favor, de onde a menina morrer?"

Tony asked the Sergeant, "What did he say?"

Sgt Avilla said, "He asks where the girl died."

Sully closed his notepad and said, "In the hospital."

Tony pulled up in front of the brownstone, and considered how he was going to tell Donald Miller that the case was closed. *"I feel like I'm telling him his daughter's dead all over again."*

"You're going to close the case? Why?" Mr. Miller clenched his teeth, and balled his hands into fists.

Tony sighed. "I don't make these decisions, Mr. Miller. I was told that, since there's no motive to do your daughter harm and no forensic evidence, there's no case. I was also told that the department has finite resources."

Mr. Miller's nostrils flared. "Finite resources? Finite resources? Well, I don't have finite resources, Detective. I'll tell you what I want you to do. I'll pay you to keep working on this case. I want you to dig deeper. I want you to get to the bottom of this. My daughter was happy and healthy… I don't suppose you have any children?"

Tony shook his head. "No, just nieces and nephews."

"And what would you do, Detective, if one of your healthy nieces or nephews was alive one minute and dead the next? Wouldn't you want to know what happened? Wouldn't you do everything in your power to find out?"

Tony held his palms out. "Believe me. I want to keep working on this case. I really do. Like I said, this wasn't my decision. I wish that there was more that I could do."

Mr. Miller pulled his phone from his pocket. "Maybe there is. I'm going to make a few calls. Don't pack it in yet Detective."

Sure enough, when Tony got back to the station, the desk sergeant told him that Captain Rodriguez wanted to see him. "He's in one hell of a mood. I'd keep your head down if I were you."

Tony said, "Thanks for the heads up."

Tony walked into his captain's office and closed the door.

Rodriguez was pacing the floor, obviously agitated, the veins in his temples clearly visible. "That guy thinks he can muscle me? When I say a case is closed, a case is closed! We've already wasted enough time and energy on this! Not to mention money; helicopters, dogs..." Captain Rodriguez sat at his desk and took a swig of coffee. "But it seems that Mr. Miller has friends in high places. Let me tell you what we're going to do. No, let me tell you what *you're* going to do." The Captain stood and jabbed his finger at Tony's chest. "YOU are going to continue this investigation ALONE! I'll give you 48 hours, and if you can't find any solid evidence, and I mean SOLID evidence, I WILL close this case. And I don't want to see you tying up ANY department resources. This department's already stretched to the limit. I don't want to spend another dime, or another man-hour on this case that I don't have to."

Tony tried to look humble. He thought that the best tactic when his captain looked like he was about to implode. He knew he shouldn't, but he couldn't resist. He asked tentatively, "Why me, Sir? Why not one of the other more experienced detectives? Why not Sully?"

Rodriguez jabbed his finger at Tony again. "Because you're the newbie. I need Sullivan to do some real police work."

Tony thought, *"Real police work, huh?"* The color rose in his cheeks and his lips pressed together in a thin red line.

As he turned to the door, Rodriguez voice stopped him as he said, "Look, Capella, This case is a joke." He held up a hand, "Don't interrupt me. It's not easy making the step to detective. We're undermanned, and what you might think of as unfair, is our reality. You have a lot of your father in you, Tony. He was like a dog that couldn't let go of a bone. I valued him for it. But there is no case here." Rodriguez looked from the papers on his desk to Tony and said, "And don't look at me like that, Capella. I valued your father. We were good friends. Just so you know; after your terrorist bust at the Red Line, I was the one who put your name in for promotion to detective."

"Sir, I…"

"But I still have a job to do. You have 48 hours Capella. Not a minute more."

Chapter 23
Do you like him?

Courtney put her pocketbook down on a chair, and two bags down on the over-bed table. Her hair was bright pink today, done up into two long ponytails. "Hey, Dee. How ya' feelin'?"

Deirdre smiled brightly. "Hey Courtney. Bring me anything good?"

Courtney opened the first bag. "Check it out." she said, as she pulled two submarine sandwiches out of the bag. "Steak and cheese for me, and I got you an Italian with the hots."

Deirdre laughed and her face turned bright red. "An Italian with the hots, huh? Funny, Court." *First it's a sweet Italian dessert, now it's an Italian with the hots.*

Courtney put her hands on Deirdre's shoulders, peered into her face and said, "Okay, tell me all about him. I want to know everything."

Deirdre blushed. "Well, he kisses really nice."

"You kissed! And you didn't tell me?"

Courtney punched Deirdre lightly on the shoulder. "Ow! What, have you been working out or something?"

"Maybe. So when did this happen? I can't believe you two made out in a hospital room."

"We didn't make out! He just kissed me. It was one kiss. Or maybe it was two kisses…"

"So tell me about him! I know he's Italian. Capella, right?"

"Yeah, Tony Capella. His brothers are all cops, and his sister is, too. He's got really nice eyes. I thought they were brown at first, but they're really more green with a little gold. I know he's a cop and everything, but I think he's a little shy."

"Shy? You've met him what, three, four times and you're already makin' out. I wouldn't call that shy." Courtney leaned forward and gave Deirdre a wicked grin.

Deirdre looked aghast. "I told you we weren't making out!" Deirdre smoothed out her bed-sheet, hung her head, and said, "The night nurse thought we were. She kicked him out of the hospital."

Courtney jumped, sending pickles from her sub across the room. "No way! Seriously?"

Deirdre chuckled. "Seriously, but it was just a kiss..." Deirdre let out a deep breath, "An awesome, fantastic kiss..."

"Yeah, right." Courtney teased. "Tell me Dee, what's he like?"

"It's hard to explain."

"Well, try."

Deirdre put her chin in her hand. "Okay, it's like, he's a man, not... not some overgrown boy trying to act like a man. He's a gentleman. I know, that sounds kind of wussy but there it is. He's a gentleman."

"Do you like him? I mean, really liiiike him?"

Deirdre looked up at the ceiling and turned red.

Courtney grinned, "Yeah, you do like him. Tell me more."

Deirdre would have liked to cross her legs, and settled instead for leaning on one elbow. "He smiles a lot..." Deirdre smiled herself at the recollection. "He's funny, well, not "funny"... he has a good sense of humor. He's makes me feel... like it's real, ya' know? There's no awkward. He like... gets me."

Courtney let out a sigh. "Wow."

"Yeah, wow is right. And what's funny is that I'm not worried about screwing it up. Isn't that nuts?"

"I'll say it again, Dee; wow."

Deirdre took a bite of her sandwich and instantly regretted it. The hot peppers were HOT! Eyes watering, she took a long pull from the straw of her drink. Courtney chuckled.

Deirdre said, "Funny Court."

Courtney sat back, slipped off her shoes and said tentatively, "Dee, um... I talked to Mrs. Geizig this morning." Courtney's eyes dropped to the floor. "She says that..."

Deirdre's unease mounted and she asked, "What is it Courtney?"

"She knows that you were hit by a car, but..." Her words tumbled over one another, "She says that if you can't come up with your share of the rent this month, that I'll have to look for another roommate. She said some other things about you being an irresponsible thrill seeker and asking what kind of person rides a bike in traffic..."

"I've been kind of freaking out about the rent. I mean, I have a little money in the bank, but the last thing I want to do is move home with my family. I mean, I pretty much just got out of there."

Courtney's eyes filled with tears "I know. I was freaking out, too. I don't want to lose my best friend as a roommate." Courtney pulled Deirdre in for a hug.

Deirdre winced at the pain from her leg, which still had a metal rod through it. She said, "Aren't there laws? I mean, she can't just kick me out, can she?"

"I don't know, Dee. Tara, from the salon, has a brother who's a lawyer, or studying to be one. I'll ask him."

"Thanks Court."

"Don't thank me. We'll figure this out, Dee."

The two friends ate in silence until Deirdre, eager to change the subject, asked, "Have you talked to my mom at all?"

Courtney rolled her eyes. "Pfft. Yeah, she said that you better not ask her for any money. Her hair was all dry, and she's looking pretty old."

"Yeah, the booze'll do that to ya'." Deirdre cocked her head to one side and said, "I don't remember ever having asked her for money. How about my brothers? I haven't had any visits from them either."

"Yeah, well, that's another thing. Your little brother, Aidan, got arrested. I didn't want to tell you, while you're in the hospital."

"What for?"

"D. U. I."

"That figures. And he just got his license."

"Hey, maybe your friend Tony can do something about it."

Deirdre's eyes shot open. "No! Absolutely not. Aidan can sit in there 'til the cows come home. I don't care. I'm not telling Tony anything about it. He knows my family's a bunch of alcoholics, but that's it. He's never gonna meet my mother or my brothers, and I'm not telling him about my father."

"Your father still down in Florida?"

"Yep. He's down there with his *new* family. The last time I called, he told me never to call again. I'm older than my 'stepmom'. Can you believe it? I'll probably have a half sister or brother any day now. Nice fam' huh?"

"Yeah, real nice. I talked to my mom last week." Courtney took another bite of her sub. "She's making you some sugar cookies. They should have been here by now. I hope she sent them 2-day mail. It's a long way from Minnesota. Hey! When you get out, ya' wanna visit my folks 'down on the farm'? It's really kinda cool, you know, in small doses, once you get used to the smell."

"Sometime. I'm gonna' have six to eight weeks of rehab when I get out of here. I talked to my boss and I hope he can put me behind a desk until my leg's better. I do have my associates in Computer Science…"

Courtney scrunched up her face in distaste. "That blows. I know how much you like sitting behind a desk or, God forbid, in a cubicle."

"Beats moving back in with mom and it wouldn't be that bad at the messenger service. There's always people coming and going. It's kind of crazy, but that's the way I like it."

"That's what I like about the salon, the *crazy*. I should probably get back. They know I'm visiting you, so it's no big deal."

As Courtney put her shoes on Deirdre said, "Thanks for coming Court. You rock."

Chapter 24
Me again

Tony sat at his mother's kitchen table, hanging his head, lost in thought. His mother smiled and placed a glass of milk in front of him. He said, "Thanks, mom. Why are you so happy?"

"You have that same look on you face your father used to get when he was on a case."

"Oh, yeah?"

"It's the same look he had when he ran into a brick wall. Tell me about it. Maybe I can help." Tony's mother took a seat opposite her son.

Tony took a drink of milk and said, "We've cleared the usual suspects. Everyone except this girl's father thinks that I'm on a wild goose chase, and I'm beginning to agree with them."

"Go on."

"There was this kid down in New Bedford... I was sure he had something to do with it, but he was in a jail cell at the time of her death."

"Really?"

"Yeah. He saved his own bacon. He asked us where, I mean *when* the victim died." Tony scratched his head. "He asked both actually... Where *and* when."

"Does that mean something?"

"I don't know... Sully answered him. He said 'In the hospital.' She died in the hospital."

Tony's mother nodded and asked, "And that means something?"

"I don't know, but maybe... maybe I've been looking in the wrong places." Tony unzipped his bag and pulled out a hospital medical record folder labeled *Nancy Miller*. He spread the papers out on the table, opposite his mother, and said, "These are the victim's medical records. Official cause of death is heart attack..." He picked up a random sheet and read it.

Tony's mother frowned at the bird's-nest-like mess of papers. She slid an EKG read-out across the table and took a look at it. Like hills and valleys, the squiggly lines of Nancy Miller's heartbeat were scrawled across the perforated graph paper. Noticing another EKG in the mass of papers, she drew it to herself, then another, and another. She lined them up along their perforated edges, shook her head, and re-shuffled them until the EKG heartbeat lines made one, continuous, readout. She nodded with satisfaction, stood and walked to a cabinet drawer. She returned with a roll of clear tape. As she pulled a length off the roll, Tony asked, "Mom, what are you doing? You just can't start taping documents together."

"This EKG is supposed to be together. Isn't it?"

"No, mom. It's from the victim's routine physicals, and her time in the ER. Look, each page is dated."

"Then why do the EKG lines line up?"

"What?"

Tony walked around the table and leaned over his mother's shoulder. "Hm..." The EKG lines lined up perfectly over the four pages, as did the lab paper's manufacturer watermark. Tony rubbed his chin and said, "This is one, continuous, EKG. Somebody split it up and labeled each page with a different date!"

"Someone at the hospital falsified the records? Why would they do that?"

"Holy-"

"Tony, language."

"I don't know, but I intend to find out." Tony got up and paced the length of the small kitchen. "I'm just not sure if I should bring this before Captain Rodriguez. He might re-evaluate the case and give me more time."

Hands on her hips, Tony's mother said, "From what you've told me, I wouldn't count on it."

"Yeah, you're right. He gave me 48 hours, and I don't want to waste them." He downed the last of his milk, kissed his mother on the forehead and said, "Thanks for the help mom!"

"Where are you off to?"

Donning his jacket as he ran out the door, he shouted, "To the hospital! You're a genius, mom!"

As the screen door banged behind her son she shook her head, smiled and said, "Yes. Yes I am."

"You again."

Tony sat himself on the corner of the hospital CEOs desk. "Yeah, me again."

"I hope you've finished your investigation, Detective. My time is not my own." If Mr. Green seemed nervous on his last visit, he was visibly sweating now.

"This guy is hiding something," thought Tony, *"but what?"*

Tony let his jacket open, just enough so that Mr. Green could see his 9 mm. Sometimes showing a gun to someone who's already nervous will make 'em slip up. "I'll let you know when I'm finished. I happen to have very little time myself. So little time in fact, that I need your personal help in getting some more medical records."

"More medical records? Do you have the proper forms? And why are you talking to me?"

Tony spread his hands, palms up. "Well, that's the thing Mr. Green. As I say, my time is limited. I need these records as soon as possible. Now, as a matter of fact. I thought we might circumvent the system somewhat. I'm sure you have access to all patient records from your computer."

"I thought we were dealing with the Miller case. What do you want? Carte blanche? HIPAA will come down on me like a ton of bricks."

"Information has come to light, Mr. Green, that implicates an employee of this hospital. It's in your best interest to cooperate."

Mr. Green's voice went up an octave as he asked quickly, "What kind of information?"

Tony thought, *"This guy has to be hiding something."* and said, "Incriminating information."

Mr. Green sat sweating for a minute before breaking the silence, "How many records are we talking about?"

"Just the records from the ER and the morgue for the last six months. That'll do."

"You want me to give you access to medical records without authorization? For a simple matter of death by heart attack?"

"I don't believe this is a simple matter. I believe this is a homicide. I'm sure that if news gets out of a homicide investigation, this hospital will have a black eye. It's a small matter to get a subpoena," Tony bluffed "but a subpoena will take time, time I don't have. I thought that we could keep this between the two of us."

Mr. Green got up and paced back and forth. "The last thing I need is bad press."

"I would think that the best way to avoid bad press would be to give me the access I need to do my job."

Mr. Green sat down at his computer, and Tony handed him a flash drive. Mr. Green looked up from his screen and said, "If word of this gets out, I could lose my job. Hell, I could be arrested. Walk lightly, Detective. I don't want a visit from the police."

Tony tucked the flash drive into his pocket. "Mr. Green, I am the police."

Tony walked up the three flights of stairs to his apartment. "Hey Chris, how're the pigeons?"

Chris was a tall, gangly 14-year-old who lived on the second floor with his single mother. A bookish kid, but nice. "Hi Tony, they're good. The babies should hatch any day now."

"That's awesome. Let me know when they do, I'd love to see them."

As Tony continued up the stairs, he made a mental note to talk to Chris' mother. *Maybe she can get him into one of those summer farm programs. He'd love that.* Tony put his key in the lock and gave it a little jiggle. Pretty much everything in his apartment needed a little jiggle: the toilet lever, the light switch in the bedroom, the kitchen faucet...

Tony put his 9 mm on the coffee table and flopped down on the couch. He reached for the TV remote, stopped, and grabbed his laptop. He slipped the flash drive with the medical records into the USB port, and a window popped up. "OK, open this file with what?"

Tony tried one program after another: UNKNOWN FILE EXTENSION. ERROR CODE.

He picked up his phone and called the computer whiz at the station. "Hey, Sean. I've got some files I can't open that I need to look at ASAP. Can I email them over to you?... Whatta' ya' mean the Captain doesn't want me tying up department resources? You're kidding me right?... Oh, that's just beautiful.... Right, thanks." *Thanks for nothing*!

Tony knew his Captain was ticked, but he couldn't believe that he'd go this far. The Captain and Nancy's father were two of a kind. They were both used to getting what they want, when they wanted it. No wonder they hated each other's guts. Tony just wished that he wasn't in the middle.

"Well, this is just great."

Tony picked up his phone and called Sully. "Hey Sully, can you believe this? I'm trying to do an investigation, and the Captain's got my hands tied behind my back... Yeah, that's just great... Yeah, wait till this blows over, right... All right, catch you later, Sully." *Unbelievable.*

Tony grabbed a can of nuts, cracked his knuckles and set down to work.

After a frustrating hour and a half of searching the web, and unsuccessfully trying all the programs he had on his computer, Tony threw in the towel. He took a quick shower, put a frozen pizza in the microwave, and grabbed the remote. As he flicked through the channels he got an idea, hit the mute button, and picked up his phone, "Hey Deirdre, it's Tony... Yeah, me too... I got a couple questions for ya'. One: Can I see you tomorrow?... Awesome. OK, two: I've got kind of a work issue, and I was wondering, do you know anything about computers?... A degree in computer science? Wow, that's impressive... That's great. I've got some files I need to look at that I can't open, and I can't do it at the station... Awesome, I'll bring my laptop by in the morning. Want me to bring you anything?... OK... I'll see you then."

Chapter 25
Spies

When Tony walked into the hospital room he found Deirdre and Courtney talking. Courtney looked up and smiled a wicked, mischievous, smile. "Hey, look who it is, the cop who got kicked out of the hospital."

Tony's faced turned scarlet. "You must be Courtney."

"And you must be Tony. You have to be a real bad-boy to get yourself kicked out of a hospital."

Tony shook his head and said. "There was nothing bad about what I did... about what happened... about what went on that night, nothing bad at all."

Tony leaned down and gave Deirdre a kiss and said, "Hey, Deirdre. I was hoping we were going to be alone."

Courtney's smiling face appeared between Tony's and Deirdre's and she asked, "Why? Ya' wanna try and get kicked out of the hospital again? Make it two for two?"

Tony asked Deirdre, "Is she always like this?"

Deirdre tapped her lips with her index finger. "Yeah, pretty much."

Courtney flopped back in her chair. "And you wouldn't have me any other way. Would ya', Dee?" Without waiting for an answer, Courtney grabbed Tony's bag. "What 'cha bring? Anything good?" She reached in and pulled out Tony's laptop. "And I was hoping for something exciting. Bummer."

Tony took the laptop from Courtney. "It might be a little bit exciting. It might be a little illegal, too. Sorry Courtney, but I really can't show you this."

"Why? Is it top secret or something?"

Tony nodded. "As a matter of fact, it is."

"Ooooooh, you're doing, like, spy stuff!" Courtney looked to Deirdre. "You're goin' to need a super cool code-name, Dee!"

Deirdre laughed. "Come on, Court."

"Ok, I get the picture. I have to get to work anyway. I'll go and let you two do your 'secret-agent' thing." Courtney picked up her bag, gave Deirdre a kiss on the forehead, and said in a low Sean Connery gravelly voice, "McDonough, Deirdre McDonough. Oh boy!"

They could hear her laughing as she went down the hall.

Tony put the laptop down next to Deirdre where she could easily see it, and cracked it open. "Okay, here's the deal. I've got less than two days to finish an investigation into the death of a young woman. I can't use any department resources, and I have to work solo."

Deirdre frowned. "What, did the police department run out of money?"

"Well, the father of the girl who died and my Captain sort of hate each other's guts. The girl's father wants a thorough investigation. My Captain feels that there's no case, and that this is a complete waste of time. But this girl's father knows people, and since I'm the low man on the totem pole, I get the short straw."

Deirdre turned the laptop towards her, took the flash drive with the medical records, and slipped it in the USB port. "Okay, let's see what we're dealing with." Deirdre tapped on the keyboard, "I've never seen this type of file. It must be some privacy thing. It shouldn't be too big a deal though. How soon do you need the information? I mean is it really important?"

"That's it, Deirdre, I won't know until I see them." Tony glanced out the door to make sure no one was standing just outside and whispered, "Okay, this has to be really hush hush. There's six months of patient medical records on that flash drive. They're from the ER of this hospital. What I really need is to find out what the patients have in common, to see if there's any link between Nancy Miller's death and any of the other patients."

Deirdre grabbed Tony's arm and whispered. "You mean someone inside this hospital killed someone in the emergency room?"

Tony squeezed back. "It's just a possibility. The likelihood is probably nil, but I promised this girl's father that I would do my best to find out how she died. Deirdre, if you don't want to do this, I understand. You'd probably be breaking at least a dozen laws by helping me."

"My friends call me Dee, ya' know."

Tony smiled and his eyes lit up. "Yeah, I know, but I like your name: 'Deirdre'. It sounds nice. I like it. So if you don't mind…"

"No, I don't mind at all, call me Deirdre."

Tony leaned down and gave Deirdre a kiss… When he got his breath back he said, "Hey, I better get going. Like I said, it's probably nothing, but just in case, don't tell anyone about this okay?"

"I won't, don't worry. I'll call you as soon as I find out anything."

Tony made his way down a long hospital hallway with brass name plates on the doors. "Here we are. He read: BARBARA HARRIS R.N. - HEAD NURSE - EMERGENCY ROOM. Tony knocked. A woman in a white lab coat opened the door and asked, "Yes?"

Tony glanced at her ID card. The picture on the card showed a Barbara Harris years younger, and much happier than the woman who stood before him. She would have been attractive, even beautiful, but her face was stern and unsmiling, her hair, graying at the temples, was pulled in a tight in a bun, and her eyes, which were blue grey, were piercing and cold. Tony flashed his badge and said, "Ms. Harris, I'm Detective Capella, with the Boston Police Department. I'd like to ask you some questions regarding the death of a Miss Nancy Miller."

"Nancy Miller…" Nurse Harris walked behind her desk. "Let me just pull her file… Yes, here it is, Nancy Miller: deceased, cause of death heart attack due to heart defect. Yes, I remember this case. It's a tragedy when a young person passes unexpectedly. I was in the E.R. when she was brought in. What did you want to know detective?"

Tony said, "I'd like to know about your colleagues actually. Do you recall if anyone in the operating room was acting strangely that day? Nervous or out of character?"

Nurse Harris looked surprised, and a little angry. She spoke with the voice of authority she'd acquired from years of practice, "Is this an internal investigation detective? As I said, I was in the operating room when Nancy Miller was brought in, and I assure you that every procedure was followed to the letter. The emergency room team that attended Miss Miller has been working together for a great deal of time. Each member of our team is top-rate, and Dr. Pritchett is our Chief of Surgery. If there has been some charge of negligence..."

"No, Ms. Harris, no charge of negligence... What about E.R. employees outside of your team? Have any of them been acting out of character?"

Nurse Harris picked up a pen, and clicked it several times. "Well... I hesitate to say this... the hospital mortician, Craig Morris, is a bit odd, more than a bit odd, to tell you the truth. I don't have any proof that he's done anything illegal, but I've heard that he... How do I put this? I heard that he 'Talks to the dead.'"

"Talks to the dead? What, like some kind of psychic medium or something?"

Nurse Harris raised one eyebrow, and Tony wondered if that were the extent of emotions she was capable of displaying. She said, "No, nothing like that. The water cooler gossip is that people have heard him talking to his 'patients', who are, incidentally, all dead... Full, one-sided conversations. Technically there's nothing wrong with that, he's not breaking any hospital rules, but still..."

Tony wrinkled his nose in disgust and said, "That's pretty creepy. Can you tell me anything else about this guy?"

"He keeps to himself. He has no friends among the

staff.   He even eats his lunch in the morgue.   Once, a janitor found him sleeping down there on one of the exam tables.   He was given a warning for that."

"Okay, super creepy.   I'll check this guy out.   Do you have his address?"

Nurse Harris tapped on her keyboard, reached under her desk, and passed Tony a sheet from her printer. Tony said, "Thanks.", handed Nurse Harris one of his cards and said, "If you think of anything else, give me a call."

Chapter 26
Porcelain dogs

Tony turned off his headlights and shut off his Jeep. He looked at his GPS, looked at the house looked at his GPS again. *What a dump. Somebody actually lives here?* He walked up the walkway, through the rusted chain-link gate and came to a rotted set of steps. He wondered if he should trust his weight on them. It looked as if he might step right through. The house looked like it hadn't been painted in 50 years. He reached through the screen door, seeing as there was no screen in it, and knocked.

A yellowed curtain in the window next to the door was pushed back a few inches and a pair of pale gray eyes, set in a long skinny face, peered out at him.

"We don't want any. Go away."

"Police, Mr. Morris. Open up."

Tony heard the rattle of a chain being drawn back from the door. The same skinny face peeked out. "Let me see your badge."

Tony pulled out his wallet and flashed his badge. "Detective Capella. Boston PD. I have a few questions for you, Mr. Morris. This will only take a few minutes. Do you mind if I come in?"

"Don't you need a warrant to come in?"

"That's right. If you want I can go get a warrant, and bring all my friends back here with me, or you can invite me in and answer my questions."

The door swung open. Tony followed Craig Morris as he walked into the living room. The house was, if anything, dirtier on the inside and more run down. It also had a strange odor, an odd smell, a sweet smell. Flowered wallpaper hung in tatters from the walls. Tony thought, *"This guy must have inherited the house from his mother, and not wanted to change a thing."* There were shelves with little porcelain dogs, and porcelain animals with little suits on, all covered with a fine layer of dust.

Mr. Morris stood in the middle of the living room, his hands straight down at his sides. The only thing he moved was his head, in an odd twitching way, like a bird. He reminded Tony of one of Chris' pigeons.

"Mr. Morris, I'm investigating the Nancy Miller case. What can you tell me about her?"

Mr. Morris rubbed his hand over his face and across his sweaty, balding forehead. "Nancy Miller… Nancy Miller… Let me think." A twisted smile spread across his face, showing yellow rotting teeth. "The secretary! What a body on that one."

Tony's eyes narrowed. He'd dealt with plenty of scum in the past. But that didn't mean they didn't tick him off. "I was hoping you could tell me something a little more relevant."

The smile faded from Craig Morris' face and turned to a look of fear when he saw how angry Tony was. "Relevant? Okay, relevant."

His head twitched. It seemed to Tony that each time he twitched he looked at the door under the stairs, the door that must lead to the basement.

"Look, I get them when they're dead. I weigh 'em, I measure 'em, I tag 'em and I bag 'em. That's it."

Mr. Morris was sweating rather more freely now. He was looking decidedly more nervous. Tony moved his forearm over his suit jacket and felt exactly where the handle of his pistol was. Just in case.

He walked over to one of the knickknack shelves and picked up a little German Shepherd.

Tony asked, "You referred to Miss Miller as 'the secretary'. How did you know that?"

"I read the papers like everybody else." Mr. Morris waved a hand at the newspaper covered coffee table.

"Did you ever meet Miss Miller before she ended up in your morgue?"

"No, I never met her."

"You ever see her?"

"No. Never."

Tony put the porcelain dog down on the coffee table and the glint of metal caught his eye. It was something round, mostly covered by a newspaper. Tony edged the newspaper aside with two fingers. It was a bracelet, a silver bangle... it was a circle of giraffes.

Tony looked from the bangle to Mr. Morris, who looked terrified. They stood looking at each other. Tony's eyes narrowed. That's when Tony heard a scratching sound. It was coming from the closed basement door. Tony started for the door and Mr. Morris blocked his path. He stretched out his arms and said, "You need a warrant to go down there, and you don't have one. You have no right."

"Get out of my way." Tony shoved Mr. Morris to the side and pulled the cellar door open. A large Siamese cat ran between Tony's legs. As Tony looked down at the cat, Mr. Morris smashed a large porcelain rabbit over the back of his head. It all happened so fast; Tony felt himself rolling down the rough wooden stairs. He didn't try to stop himself, instead he went with it, and rolled to his feet when he hit the ground.

The mortician slammed into Tony just as he was getting his bearings. Tony went crashing into a wall, his cell phone slipping from his pocket. Tony lunged off his back foot and struck with double open palms to Morris' chest. Morris flew backwards. His calves caught the edge of a low table, and he fell over on his back with a loud thud.

Tony looked around the basement room. It looked like a scene from hell. All over the walls were pictures... pictures of naked people... dead people, some lying flat, and some in bizarre poses; some were old, some were young. Tony wanted to throw up. On a narrow table against one wall was what looked to be a dead, dried up spider. With revulsion Tony realized that it was a severed human hand.

Morris was back on his feet. "Ahhhhh!" he screamed. His eyes were wide, and spittle flew from his mouth. "I'll kill you!"

He ran forward, arms outstretched, his hands looking like claws. Just as he was within range Tony delivered a front snap kick to his jaw. Tony heard the sound of bone breaking.

While anyone else would have stayed down, Morris got up again. In his rage, he was beyond pain, and beyond reason. Mr. Morris charged again... *When something extremely scary is coming straight at you, with the goal of doing you great personal harm, you have two choices; you can fall apart and cry like a little baby, or you can meet it head on.* Tony's adrenaline redlined, he pulled his 9 mm and shouted, "Come on!" as he leveled his gun at Morris' head.

Either the gun or the shout stopped Morris in his tracks. He stood stock still, then, incredibly fast, he reached down, grabbed the edge of the small table and flung it at Tony's face. As Tony blocked the table with his forearms, Morris turned and fled up the stairs.

Deirdre tapped the keys on her laptop, her left index finger hovering over the F9 key, which would bring up a page on mountain bikes, in case anyone one happened to come in. Deirdre thought, *"This should be easier."*

Correlating information brought her back to her days spent in a cubicle. *Like a good little hamster.* It didn't help that the files wouldn't work with her software. *The hospital must have some weird operating system.* She'd had to find and download a program to convert all the files. And she'd had to do it between people changing the sheets, nurses taking her temperature and blood pressure, and the 'Jell-O wagon' that brought her cardboard meals three times a day. The pain medication didn't make it any easier either. *Traffic is light tonight,* she thought, *A baseball game must be on.*

While Deirdre waited for yet another program to

download, she thought about Tony. It must be exciting being a detective, running down leads, questioning suspects... Deirdre tried to picture herself in a police uniform. *I can't be a bike messenger forever... maybe a bicycle cop?* She'd get to ride all day, in good weather anyway. *What do bicycle cops do in the winter? I'll have to ask Tony.*

I wonder what Tony's doing right now. He said he was working solo, and Deirdre hadn't liked that a bit. *I'm sure he can take care of himself, I mean, he has a gun, but still...* Deirdre closed her eyes and formed a mental image of Tony in a dark alley, with his gun drawn, and his hair tussled... looking handsome, and brave... The image changed from Tony the cop to Tony the barber, with a white apron and mustache... that made her smile. Then followed Tony the fireman, Tony the Lumberjack... Deirdre let out a deep breath. She had to admit, she liked Tony the cop best. *Can I see myself as a cop? Maybe doing computer work for the police would be more exciting than sitting in a cubicle, I mean I do have my degree in computer science...* She wondered what her family would say, and found that she didn't care. It wouldn't matter to Courtney what she did. She knew just what Courtney would say about her being a cop, "Whatever floats your boat, Dee, just don't sell used cars."

Deirdre watched the loading bar on the laptop go from 98%... 99%... 100%. DOWNLOAD COMPLETE. She opened the program. *"Maybe I'll get somewhere with this one..."*

Gun in hand, Tony bolted up the stairs after the mortician. At the top landing, he swung around the doorframe, his pistol scanning the room, to make sure it was clear. He heard a clatter from outside the open front door. Morris crashed through some of the debris in his front yard. Tony bolted through the living room, across the porch, and over the front steps. It was pitch dark. Holding his gun in both hands, Tony swept left to right, then right to left.

The houses in the neighborhood where tightly packed together. A dog barked off to Tony's right, so he headed towards it. Tony heard the sound of breaking glass, followed by the scream of a woman. He ran between two houses towards the sound. As he got closer he could distinguish words. "Get out of my house! Get out of my house!"

Tony ran in the open back door to find Morris and a 250-pound woman wrestling over a set of car keys. When the woman saw Tony in the doorway, in his suit and tie, with his gun drawn, she released the keys. When Mr. Morris turned and saw a gun pointed at his face, he stopped wide-eyed and looked about the kitchen. On the counter was a knife rack. Morris took two steps towards it. With his free hand, Tony grabbed him from behind by the hair and drove a side-kick downwards behind his knee. Tony's adrenaline was up, and he wasn't about to mess around. He drove the morticians face into the sticky linoleum floor, put a knee on his back and cuffed him.

"Craig Morris, you're under arrest. You have the right to remain silent. Anything you say may be used against you in a court of law." Tony held the chain of the handcuffs in one hand.

Craig Morris looked up at Tony, again with his twisted smile, and said, "I know it's against the law, but it's just defacing a corpse. That's six months to a year, max."

Tony jerked Morris to his feet by the handcuffs. "That's true, but aren't you forgetting something?"

"What?"

"Attempted murder of a police officer. That's more like 20 to life."

Chapter 27
Commonalities

Deirdre crossed her fingers, and hit ENTER. The program she was using was either very old, or very primitive. The results of the cross-index came up in white on a green screen. *Very 1982.*

Commonalities 556 records: 100% match (5) records:
Non-smoker
Drug use: negative
List of prescription medications: none
History of hereditary disease: negative
History of genetic deformity: negative
Prior surgeries: none
Age: 22 to 26 years
Physical condition: excellent
Blood type: *AB-
Organ donor: yes

List chronological by name:

Marie Blanc   patient number 472935
*AB-

                               Status: deceased organ
                               donor: liver and kidneys

Peter Higgins   patient number 473012
*AB-

                               Status: deceased organ
                               donor: eyes and lungs

Olivia Ferguson *AB-	patient number 473219
	Status: deceased organ donor: heart
Nancy Miller *AB-	patient number 473565
	Status: deceased organ donor: kidneys
Deirdre McDonough *AB-	patient number 473636
	Status: organ donor: awaiting treatment

Deirdre put her hand over her mouth and gasped, her heart caught in her throat. *"Oh God, oh God."* She stared at her name glowing white in the darkened room. She closed her eyes and tried to calm herself and to slow her rapid breathing. She feared someone might hear it.

Like a cornered animal her flight instincts kicked in. She grabbed the rail of the hospital bed and tried to pull herself up. The pain of the metal rod through her leg reminded her that she wasn't going anywhere on her own. She let out a gasp of pain. *"Five patients with a 100% match. Four of them are dead… All organ donors… I'm next. Oh God, I'm next."* She grabbed her phone off the bedside table and had to dial twice, her hands were shaking so badly. A message played: "Hello, you've reached the voice mailbox of Detective Tony Capella. Please leave your name and number and a brief message at the sound of the tone."

A shadow fell over Deirdre. She looked up, eyes wide with fright, into the face of a nurse.

"I thought I heard someone cry out. What's wrong? Can't sleep?" The nurse walked over to the monitor beside

Deirdre's bed. "Your blood pressure is quite elevated, and your pulse is very rapid."

Deirdre's mind raced as she scrambled to think of an explanation.

The nurse looked down at the open laptop. Deirdre thought, *"Did she see the screen?"*

In her panic, she'd forgotten all about the F9 key, which would pull up an innocent web page. Deirdre quickly closed the laptop and said, "I, um, I had a bad dream… just… just a bad dream. I'm all right."

"Can I get you a glass of water, dear?"

"Sure, yeah, okay thanks."

As the nurse went to get a glass of water, Deirdre thought, *"Should I tell the nurse? Can I trust anyone in this place? No, no way. I'll try Tony again once she leaves."*

The nurse came back into the room carrying a plastic carafe with ice water and a glass, and said, "Here you are dear" as she put the carafe down on the table and handed Deirdre the glass. As Deirdre took a drink, she read the nurse's nametag. Barbara Harris R.N. As the nametag slipped out of focus, Deirdre slipped into unconsciousness.

Tony dragged the mortician into the police station. "Hey Murph', do me a solid and throw this scumbag in a cell. You might want to call medical, I think there's something wrong with his jaw, and probably his knee."

Tony walked into the bathroom, and splashed some water on his face. He looked in the mirror and turned his head from side to side. He had a good bruise on his right cheekbone and a cut through his left eyebrow. He ran his fingers through his hair to try and make himself a little more presentable. *"Yeah, right,"* he thought, *"As if that's gonna' happen."*

He was filthy.

Capt. Rodriguez was gone for the night so Tony went to look for the Duty Sergeant. As Tony walked down the hall, Sean, the self proclaimed 'lab rat' ran up behind him and called out, "Hey Tony, you gotta' sec'?"

Tony rolled his eyes. He hadn't forgotten how Sean had blown him off when he needed his help. "Is it important?"

Sean nodded. "You'll want to see this."

Tony followed Sean down to the lab, and sat down in front of a monitor with a video paused on the screen. Sean leaned over Tony's shoulder. "I looked at that video from the coffee shop, the one with that totally hot girl. I mean, the video you asked me to look at, and I didn't find anything. Then I was showing it to some of the guys, you know..." Sean blushed. "I was standing behind them while we watched, and I don't know, maybe because I was looking from another angle, I saw this..." Sean reached over Tony's shoulder and pressed play.

"What am I looking at Sean? I've had kind of a long day so..."

Sean tapped the keyboard and clicked the mouse; zooming in on the front window of the coffee shop. "Watch the reflection."

Tony watched the reflected image, and saw a woman putting something in Nancy Miller's coffee. "Can you zoom in on that woman's face? Can you make it any clearer?"

"I should be able to. The video quality is surprisingly good... Hold on... Let me increase the contrast... And still frame. How's that?"

"That's... That's Nurse Harris!"

Tony reached into his pocket for his phone, "Damn! I must have dropped it chasing Morris. Sean, I need you to do a few things for me. First, give me your cell phone."

"My cell phone?"

"And I need you to send a couple of squad cars over to the mortician's house to check all the closets."

"All the closets?"

"Closets, any out-buildings, they have to be checked over from top to bottom to see if there's anybody tied up."

"Anybody tied up?"

Tony wrote the address down and passed it to Sean. "You heard me. Now give me your damn cell phone." Sean passed it over.

Tony dialed Deirdre as he ran out the door. "Come on Deirdre, pick up…pick up…   Damn it!" Tony dialed another number. "Sully, I need you to meet me over at the hospital now!… You wouldn't believe me if I told you. My girlfriend was helping me on the Miller case, I can't get her on the phone, and Deirdre's nurse is the same one who killed Nancy Miller. I'm driving over there now… Right, see you there."

Tony jumped into his Jeep and hit the gas. He hit the flashing lights in the grill and turned on the siren. Tony's jeep literally flew out of the underground parking garage. Tires screeched as he turned onto the main drag.

Chapter 28

Not again

"Not again!" Deirdre woke up and took a look at her surroundings. "Okay, where am I now?"

She was in a wheelchair, backed into the corner of a brightly lit room. When she went to move, she found to her horror that her arms were duct-taped to the arms of the wheelchair. "Oh, my God."

Her leg was in agony. She looked down and saw the metal rod that had once been suspended was still sticking out of her leg. She grimaced and let out an agonized moan.

"I'd give you something for the pain dear, but I don't see any need. You'll be dead soon enough." Nurse Harris walked into the room and put her hands on Deirdre's. She brought her face to within inches of hers and said, "Let's see, how are you going to die? A blood clot? We need to put something on your death certificate. That happens all the time. Pity."

Deirdre looked to the door and screamed, "Help! Help me, please!"

Nurse Harris joined in mockingly, "Help! Help!" and then in a normal voice, "Yell all you want. Nobody's going to hear you."

Deirdre's chest rose and fell with deep lungfuls of air. Her nostrils flared. "Why? Why are you doing this? Aren't there enough organ donors?"

"Oh, there are donors. Anyone can buy organs on the black market, but you're a *perfect* donor. We'll get a hundred times the money for your organs. Actually, your blood type is AB-; only 1% of the world's population has AB-, so we'll get a thousand times the money from you." Nurse Harris smiled, "You're quite the little cash cow. Everybody wins. I get lots of money. The hospital wins…" Nurse Harris waved her arm at the monitors and other equipment in the room, "This equipment doesn't come cheap, and organ transplantation is expensive."

Deirdre struggled violently and the wheelchair moved a few inches. "Struggle all you want dear. We don't need your arms."

Deirdre looked about wildly for a means of escape. "Tony, I mean Detective Capella will be here soon. He knows all about this."

"I don't think so. I sent your Detective boyfriend on a wild goose chase. Right now he's probably having a nice little chat with our psychotic mortician. Besides, he wouldn't find us here anyway. We're in the new medical wing of the hospital. It's still under construction, and not set to open until next month. This operating suite was only just finished."

Deirdre needed time to think. She asked, "How many people are in on this?"

Nurse Harris looked at her fingernails. "Oh, just enough: myself, the good Doctor... the Head Toxicologist. You'd be surprised what a pay raise and a trip to the Bahamas can accomplish."

"The Toxicologist?"

"Well, we can't have loved ones finding out that their dearly departed have been given a nice little cocktail, can we? I've been very busy myself, slipping something into someone's drink so that they might have to take a trip to the emergency room... It's almost like mail order. Brings them right to your door... And it's so much cleaner than other methods."

"You murdered all those people."

"Murder? I see people die every day, sweetie. Might as well make a profit from it."

"You're sick!"

Nurse Harris walked over to an instrument tray and picked up a scalpel. "You didn't happen to notice the driver of the car that hit you?" she asked with a grin.

That got Deirdre angry. "You bitch! You rotten bitch! You took my life away from me!"

Nurse Harris laughed. "Yes I did, and I will, again, very soon and permanently." She smoothed the wrinkles in her lab coat and took out her phone. "That's right. There's no signal in the new wing. No matter. I'll be right back, and we can get this party started. The sooner we're done with you, the sooner I can sit back on a beach with a margarita."

Nurse Harris put the scalpel down on the tray, and walked out of the operating suite.

Deirdre heard Nurse Harris' footsteps recede and thought, *"I have to move."*

She rocked her body back and forth and slowly hobbled the wheelchair towards the instrument tray. Each movement sent a jolt of pain up her injured leg. Deirdre looked down and saw a trickle of blood flowing around her metal rod. When she was close enough, she hooked the toes of her good leg around the pole of the instrument cart, and pulled it towards herself. "If I can just get hold of a scalpel…"

She moved slowly… her hands were shaking… she almost had it… the tray started to slip… "Oh no."

Just as she grasped the scalpel with the tips of two fingers, the tray crashed to the floor. Deirdre looked at the door thinking that Nurse Harris must've heard that. She brought the scalpel blade down towards her forearm and started cutting the duct tape. When she had cut about 2 inches, she twisted her arm and heard a satisfying rip as the duct tape tore free. She switched the scalpel to the other hand and cut. Now both of her arms were free.

Deirdre tucked the scalpel beside her thigh and wheeled herself out the door. Naked bulbs created pools of light spaced 30 feet apart in the dark, half finished, hospital wing. Stacks of sheet rock, metal studs and spools of wire littered the scene. Nurse Harris had taken a left when she walked out the door, so Deirdre steered herself right.

Dr. Pritchett stepped off the elevator to find Nurse Harris waiting for him. "Nurse." he said.

Nurse Harris replied, "Doctor," in a very professional manner.

Dr. Pritchett walked to Nurse Harris, grabbed her bottom with both hands, and kissed her passionately.

"Why Doctor, that might be constituted as sexual harassment."

"I'll show you sexual harassment when we're done with our patient."

Nurse Harris smiled an evil smile. "Our patient's strapped into a wheelchair. Maybe we should make her watch?"

Dr. Pritchett returned her smile. "Kinky. Very kinky. I like it."

They entered the surgical suite side-by-side, and found it empty. Nurse Harris jaw dropped. She looked left and right, to the corners of the empty room, before exclaiming, "That little bitch!"

Dr. Pritchett turned and slapped her across the face. "You idiot! Find her!" Dr. Pritchett looked down at the floor and saw pieces of duct tape and drops of blood. "She's bleeding. Find her!" As they raced out of the surgical suite, Dr. Pritchett said, "You go this way, I'll go this way" and strode off to the left, to leave Nurse Harris to search the right.

It took Nurse Harris only minutes to find fresh blood gleaming like red jewels under the construction lights. She called out, "Deirdre?... Deirdre?... Come out, come out, wherever you are..."

Tony wove around the few cars on the road, and a pedestrian who was too drunk to get out of the way. It was late, so traffic was light, made up chiefly by delivery trucks, and early morning work crews. As Tony barreled down Washington Street, he came up fast on an SUV in the left lane. The driver stayed on the left, totally oblivious. When Tony went to pass on the right, the driver, who Tony saw was texting, finally saw the blue lights. Probably thinking that she was being stopped, she pulled hard to the right, forcing Tony over. Tony 'threaded the needle' and clipped half a dozen side mirrors from the cars parked along the street, as well as his own. Tony yelled, "Idiot!" over his shoulder and hit the gas.

Traffic lights went by in a blur as he drove. His right wheel shuddered violently as he hit a deep pothole, and he wondered what damage he'd done to his front end.   He knew he'd done something to his exhaust, it was loud!

Tony blew through the intersections, one after another. He skidded up to the Emergency Room entrance, pulled on the emergency brake, and raced inside.

Deirdre found a staircase and pulled frantically at the door, only to find it locked. *"Well, I probably would have broken my neck trying stairs anyway."* she thought.

The floors were bare concrete in the section of the new wing. Pieces of sheet rock and metal studs hindered her progress. It was slow going in her wheelchair, and several times she had to backtrack when she hit a dead end. She wheeled herself to a row of windows overlooking the dark city street, seven stories down. *None of them open. And even if they did, what good would it do me?*

Deirdre had never been in a fight. She preferred to use words over violence; in High School, shopping on black Friday, it had always worked… *'Till now. If I don't find a way out soon, I'll have no choice but to face these psychos.* She looked at her reflection in one of the windows. She looked small, weak and vulnerable. She thought, *"I probably couldn't fight my way out of a wet paper bag right now… I wish Tony were here."* Deirdre's face brightened at the thought of Tony. *"But how would he even know I'm here*?" Deirdre started to choke up when she thought that there was a very good possibility she'd be dead before morning. "*And I just met him... It isn't fair.*" She felt the tears start to flow. "*No.*" She frowned. "*That's not happening. Pull it together, McDonough.*"

Deirdre gritted her teeth and pushed her wheelchair through a patch of dust and trash. She searched for another door and found nothing, only more rubbish and construction debris. Electrical cables across the jarred the wheelchair, sending waves of pain through her injured leg. She was sweating freely, even as a cold breeze made her shiver in her light hospital gown. She steered herself to a dark corner and stopped behind a pallet of ceiling tiles, breathing hard. She looked around, trying to find some sort of weapon, a length of pipe or a hammer, anything.

Nurse Harris followed the trail of blood droplets. "*Just like Hansel and Gretel,*" she thought. She rubbed her cheek where Dr. Pritchett had slapped her. "Bastard." She was angrier with herself then with Dr. Pritchett, and it wasn't the first time he'd struck her. "How could I have let that little bitch get away? Wait till I find her..." She followed the blood trail to a staircase door. When Nurse Harris turned the handle she found it locked. "Well, that makes my life easier."

Once again, she found the blood trail. She followed the drops towards the corner where Deirdre was hiding. She approached the pallets slowly, and in the dim light caught a glimpse of steel from the wheelchair. "What a naughty, naughty patient I have. Do you know what we do to naughty patients?"

Deirdre backed away in her wheelchair, but she wasn't fast enough for Nurse Harris, who strode forward and kicked Deirdre in the shin of her injured leg. Deirdre screamed and arched her back in agony, her knuckles white on the arms of the wheelchair.

"Try anything like that again and I'll pull that metal rod out, and I'll do it nice and slowly."

Deirdre sagged back into the chair and took a few deep, labored breaths. As the spasms of pain receded, Deirdre felt the handle of the scalpel pressing against her thigh. She reached down slowly and grasped it. As Nurse Harris walked towards the back of the wheelchair to push Deirdre, Deirdre lunged and drove the scalpel deep into Nurse Harris' thigh. Nurse Harris screamed and fell over sideways grasping at her leg as she rolled from side to side on the floor.

Deirdre was on the move. All thoughts of hiding forgotten, she concentrated on speed. With bloody hands, she turned the wheels of her chair as hard as she could, determined to put as much distance between Nurse Harris and herself as possible. She raced straight down the hallway looking desperately for a way out. As she came to an intersection, she stopped and looked left and right. Out of the shadows stepped Dr. Pritchett.

"Hello Deirdre. You were almost late for your appointment."

Deirdre's heart died in her chest. "Stay away from me!" she screamed.

She backed her wheelchair furiously, and was brought up short by a concrete pillar.

"Stay away from me!"

"It's a little late for that, don't you think? Have you seen my colleague, Nurse Harris?" A mute Deirdre stared up at Dr. Pritchett, who gazed down at the blood covering her hands and splattered over her hospital gown. "I see that you have. It seems that you have quite upset my plans young lady. Now, what to do with you? Kill you now and depart? Or should I operate first?"

Dr. Pritchett looked at his watch.

When Tony got to Deirdre's room he found her bed empty. "Damn it! Where can they have taken her?" Tony felt his chest tighten as a sense of panic and dread started to take hold. That's when his police training kicked in. He ran to the elevator and looked at the floor map of the hospital. He punched in the first floor and made his way to the security office. A woman pushing a cart of fresh linen stared as he raced past.

Tony found the door marked 'Hospital Security', yanked it open, and raced down a narrow hall. At the end of the hall was a plexi-glass window with a circular cut-out, and next to it a call button. Tony kept his finger on the button, and half a minute later a guard came to the window. Tony flashed his badge at the guard behind the glass. "Detective Capella, Boston P.D. I need to see your security camera footage for the last hour or so, and I need to see it NOW."

The guard buzzed Tony in and quickly brought him to the video control room. Seated in front of a panel of video screens was a middle-aged man, with close-cropped hair in a trim security uniform. Tony thought, *"Ex-military, probably army."*

The first guard introduced them, "David this Detective Capella. He needs to see some video footage pronto."

The guard calmly looked up and said, "Okay, date, time and floor?"

Tony said, "Today, fifth floor, from 11:30, I mean 2300 hours 'till now."

The security guard knew his stuff and started rolling a trackball through the footage. Tony could picture this guy on a battlefield directing troops.

Tony leaned in. "There, stop right there." The video stopped on a black-and-white image of a nurse pushing a wheelchair. *That has to be Deirdre.* "Okay, can you see where they're going?"

The guard pulled up an image of multiple video screens. "Right, okay, camera 6... There, got 'em."

The guard switched cameras, and from this angle it was clear that Deirdre was in the wheelchair. Nurse Harris and

Deirdre disappeared into an elevator.

Tony made a fist. "Where does that elevator go?"

"It goes to the new medical wing. There aren't any cameras installed there yet. Well, they're installed but they're covered because they kept getting filled with dust from the construction."

Tony pointed at the first security guard. "What's your name?"

"Mike."

"Mike, you're coming with me."

Tony sprinted down the hall with Mike on his heels. "What's going on?"

Tony didn't have the patience, or the breath for a long explanation. He said, "Good guy, bad guy stuff. Just keep up!"

When they got to the elevator Tony took off his jacket and tie, shoved them into Mike's arms and said, "Okay, Mike. You stay here and wait for my partner, Detective Sullivan."

The last thing Tony needed was an unarmed security guard to look after. "If anyone but me gets out of this elevator, don't let them leave. I don't care if it's the Pope. Understand? Don't let them leave."

The floor indicator said that the elevator was on the 7th floor. Tony drew his 9 mm and said, "Tell Sully I'm on the 7th floor, and to expect trouble."

The guard nodded, Tony stepped into the elevator and pressed the button for the 7th floor.

When the doors opened, Tony knelt down, looked around the corner and swept the hallway. It was empty.

Chapter 29
Let the girl go

Dr. Pritchett walked casually over to Deirdre. He opened his mouth to speak, thought better of it, and closed it again. He stood and looked down at her, his face devoid of emotion save for a vein pulsing in his neck. Without preamble, he backhanded her across the face. "Oh!" she cried. Her head snapped back and the wheelchair fell over on its side, spilling Deirdre onto the floor and knocking the wind out of her. He reached down, grabbed a fistful of her short blond hair, and dragged her down the hall. Deirdre thrashed and kicked out. She reached up with both hands and grabbed his wrist. Deirdre screamed, "No, no, let me go! Stop!"

Dr. Pritchett jerked Deirdre violently up by the hair and pulled her so close that she could feel his breath on her face. Dr. Pritchett snarled and said, "If you don't shut up, the first thing I'll cut out of you will be your tongue."

"Not if I shoot you in the face." Tony walked out of the shadows towards Dr. Pritchett, his gun drawn. "Let the girl go. Step away, and get face-down on the floor."

Dr. Pritchett let go of Deirdre's hair and put his hands up as high as his shoulders. He made no move to get down on the floor. Tony walked over, grabbed Dr. Pritchett by the hair, and pulled him down backwards. He hit the concrete floor with a resounding thud. Tony put the barrel of his 9mm to Dr. Pritchett's temple, and through gritted teeth said, "I told you to get down on the floor you filthy piece of…"

"Now, now Detective. That type of language is not permitted in this hospital."

Tony looked over his left shoulder. Nurse Harris was on her knees, the lower half of her lab coat soaked in her own blood. She had her left arm around Deirdre's throat, and held a bloody scalpel in her right hand, level with Deirdre's eyes.

"Drop the gun, Detective." she said in an unnervingly calm voice. "To my recollection, I've assisted in 37 eye transplant operations. That makes for a total of 148 eyes that I've seen cut out of patient's heads. It seems quite simple, really, and I've always wanted to try. A simple twist of the wrist... Should I start with your pretty little girlfriend?"

Tony looked into Nurse Harris' cold blue eyes, and didn't like what he saw there. In karate tournaments he'd faced black belts who'd do anything to win, so they wouldn't "embarrass" their watching students. He'd taken down drug dealers who'd do anything not to go back to prison. They had had the same look in their eyes as he was seeing now. Tony looked down with contempt at Dr. Pritchett, and flicked his gun down the hallway. It was one thing to lose your weapon; it was another to arm your enemy.

"Good." said Dr. Pritchett, as he got up off the floor. He dusted off his lab coat, walked over to the wheelchair, and set it back on its wheels. "Barbara, can you walk? I believe it's time for us to make our exit."

Nurse Harris nodded, her face as pale as milk. "I put a dressing on the wound this little bitch gave me. It should be fine for now. You can look at it later."

Dr. Pritchett picked Deirdre up under the arms, and sat her in the wheelchair. She gasped in pain as the rod struck the side of the chair. Her left eye was purple and swollen shut from the punch, there was a film of blood over her teeth, and her chin was scraped raw. Deirdre looked at Tony as if to ask: *"What should I do?"* Tony put his palm down, signaling Deirdre to *"wait"*. He didn't want her to try anything, especially in her weakened condition.

A bell chimed down the hall as the elevator doors opened. Dr. Pritchett looked to Tony. "Are you expecting someone? Don't make a sound," Dr. Pritchett took the scalpel from Nurse Harris and pointed it at Deirdre, "or Miss McDonough will be in need of a new face."

Dr. Pritchett and Nurse Harris had a whispered conversation, and Dr. Pritchett slipped her something, which she tucked into her lab-coat pocket. Nurse Harris smiled and nodded, then headed down the hall towards the elevator.

When Sully got Tony's call, he was sitting on the couch, watching TV with his wife. Sully might have a trunk full of ratty old sweatshirts, some of which he liked to wear on weekends, but you wouldn't know it from looking at his house. His wife, Brenda, kept every surface meticulously clean. Most of their furniture was old wood, which Brenda kept polished and oiled. Pictures of their kids, nieces and nephews, in graduation caps and gowns, having snowball fights and playing little league covered one wall.

Sully hung up the phone, yawned, stretched, kissed his wife on the cheek, and said, "I gotta run into work honey. Be back in a bit." as if he was going down to the corner market for a gallon of milk.

Sully's wife wasn't fooled at all, as Sully slipped his arm through his shoulder holster she said, "Make sure it's loaded, and keep your head down."

He gave her a mock salute, double checked his .45 and said, "I always do." He gave his wife a wink and a kiss, said, "Love ya'." and walked out the door.

Sully lived closer to the hospital, and had a shorter drive than Tony. He shook his head when he found Tony's jeep, lights flashing, parked in front of the emergency room entrance. Even though he'd driven like a madman, Tony had beaten him.

When Sully couldn't reach Tony on his borrowed cell phone, he made his way to Deirdre's room and found it empty. Like Tony, he made his way to hospital security. When he was told about the video of Nurse Harris pushing

Deirdre, he made a call to the station for backup, and then jogged down to the new wing, where he found, Mike, the security guard waiting for him.

In halting sentences, Mike relayed to Sully everything Tony had told him. There was a quaver in Mike's voice as he said, "Looks like the action's on the 7th floor."

Sully said, "Stay put, and under no circumstances come up. Back-up should be here soon."

Mike nodded. As Sully stepped into the elevator, he could see from the look on Mike's face that he had no intention of coming up. As the doors closed, Sully saw Mike turn and walk briskly away, back up the hallway. Sully shook his head. *Whimp. Go find another job*" he thought. Sully had no patience with cowardice. You could teach a man how to shoot, and how to obey orders, but you couldn't teach them how to be brave.

Sully stepped out of elevator with his .45 drawn, and made his way slowly down the hall, scanning as he went. He stopped and shifted his aim as a nurse, covered in blood, came staggering around the corner. "Help me, please!" she cried as she stumbled towards him.

Sully caught her with his free arm as she slumped to the floor. He asked, "What happened? Who did this to you?"

On one knee, cradling Nurse Harris with his left arm, Sully looked over her shoulder through his gun sights down the hall.

Nurse Harris slipped the syringe from her pocket, and thrust it with all her might at Sully's exposed throat.

Tony stood in the hall, his eyes wide and his heart beating loudly in his chest. "Let the girl go, Doctor."

Dr. Pritchett raised an eyebrow. "Or what, you'll kill me?"

"The thought had crossed my mind." Tony looked to Deirdre. Light reflected off the blade of the scalpel, an inch from her face. "Deirdre, I'm sorry. I shouldn't have gotten you into this."

Deirdre, one eye swollen closed, blood steadily seeping from the rod through her leg, tried to smile as she said, "And to think this morning I was complaining about being bored." She bit her lip. "I'm really glad I met you, Tony. I want you to know that. Just… just in case…"

"Don't talk like that! We're not done yet."

Tony heard footsteps coming from the direction of the elevator. Around the corner came Sully and Nurse Harris. Sully had Nurse Harris' arm pinned behind her back, and was none too gently pushing her forward. "Hey, Tony."

Tony exhaled. "Hey, Sully. Good to see ya'."

Sully took in the situation at once. "Okay, shows over. Let her go."

Dr. Pritchett moved the scalpel closer to Deirdre's face and simply said, "No."

Tony slowly walked over and stood beside Sully. He glared at Dr. Pritchett and said, "We'll trade. Let the girl go, and we'll trade."

Dr. Pritchett sighed. "I think not."

Sully put his .45 to Nurse Harris' temple and cocked the hammer. "We trade or I put a bullet through her head. How's that for motivation?"

Dr. Pritchett looked almost amused. "Go ahead. She means nothing to me. Now, if you'll excuse me I must be going."

Dr. Pritchett swung the wheelchair and headed backwards toward the elevator, keeping Deirdre in front of him for cover, and the scalpel at her throat. Tony, Sully, and Nurse Harris, still in Sully's arm-lock, followed behind.

Tony whispered through clenched teeth, "Sully!"

Sully whispered back, "Easy kid, I got this."

Dr. Pritchett backed the wheelchair into the elevator and stood behind Deirdre. He pressed the elevator button, and grinned. As the doors started to close, Dr. Pritchett said,

"Goodbye, detectives… Goodbye, Barbara."

Just as the elevator doors touched, Sully released his hold on Nurse Harris, aimed, and fired two shots. Two holes appeared in the elevator doors, near the seam where they met. As the sounds of Sully's shots echoed off the bare concrete walls, Tony ran forward and pressed the elevator call button. He watched the digital read-out go from the seventh floor down to the first, then back up to the seventh. It was the longest minute of Tony's life.

When the doors opened, Deirdre wheeled herself out of the elevator, leaving two tracks of red. Dr. Pritchett was laying in a pool of blood, with one hole in his cheek, the other through his eye. Sully walked in and nudged the doctor with the toe of his shoe. "See kid, .45. Nothin' beats a .45 for penetration."

Tony walked over and wrapped his arms around Deirdre. "Deirdre, this is my partner Sully. Sully, this is Deirdre."

As Sully was putting the handcuffs on Nurse Harris he said, "Nice to meet you, Deirdre. Tony, this one's a keeper."

Chapter 30
As in Florida?

Tony didn't leave Deirdre's bedside the following week. Courtney popped in and out for visits, and at one point shoved an armload of soaps and hair care products into Tony's arms, pushed him into the bathroom for a much needed shower and said, "Get in there. I'll stand guard."

When Courtney heard the water running for the shower, she turned to Deirdre and, in her best Sean Connery impression, said, "McDonough, Deirdre McDonough.".

Deirdre laughed and said, "Will you *please* stop saying that!"

Courtney laughed. "It fits now doesn't it?"

Deirdre ran her hand over her knee. Free from the metal rod, it was freshly bandaged but extremely sore. Courtney said, "I can't believe they gave Tony a week's vacation! He's only been a detective for like a week!"

Deirdre smiled and said, "Actually... They gave him a month's vacation."

Courtney's eyebrows shot up. "Get out! A month! You're kidding, right?"

"Nope, full pay and everything. The mayor personally put in for the vacation. It's good for his popularity, having a hero on the police force. The whole 'murder in the E. R.' thing has gone viral. They've been after Tony all week to put in appearances on morning TV shows, but he wants to see me better first."

Courtney said, "Dee, you should totally go on TV with Tony. I heard you can make a lot of money on those morning shows."

Deirdre nodded and said, "I heard that, too. Maybe we will when we get back."

With a puzzled look, Courtney asked, "Get back? Get back from where?"

Deirdre smiled and looked up at the ceiling.

Courtney was stunned. "No way! No flippin' way! Deirdre! Oh my gosh! Oh my gosh! You're getting married!?"

Deirdre nodded quickly and said, "Yup. And I need a maid of honor. You wouldn't know anyone who'd like to be a maid of honor would you?"

Courtney shrieked at the top of her lungs, "Yes! Oh my gosh! Yes! And we have to pick out a dress, and there's the flowers... Are you going to get married in a church?" Courtney spun on the spot and shouted, "My best friend is getting married!"

Deirdre heard the rattle of the bathroom doorknob. Tony leaned out the doorway with a towel wrapped about his waist and said excitedly, "What's the matter? What's goin' on? Who screamed?"

Courtney grabbed Tony on either side of his head, kissed him on both cheeks and said, "You're marrying my best friend! That makes us like... that makes you like my brother-in-law!"

Tony rolled his eyes, shook his head and said, "Totally, Courtney. Totally."

When Tony, showered, shaved and fully dressed, stepped out of the bathroom toweling his hair, he was surprised to find the room full of people, including reporters and cameramen from channels 4 and 7.

Sully patted him on the back and said, "Tony, Tony, Tony... What am I gonna do with you? I told you to find a nice girl, but geez Louise, you're moving a little fast, aint cha?"

Tony walked over, held Deirdre's hand and said, "When something totally awesome is coming straight at you, you have two choices; you can fall apart and cry like a little baby, or you can meet it head on." Tony and Deirdre smiled at Sully.

A knocking on the door made the three turn to see who was there. Donald Miller stood in the doorway. He took in the television cameras and the smiling faces. He cleared his throat and, in a soft voice that was quite out of character, asked, "Is this a bad time?"

Tony adopted a more serious expression and said, "Of course not, Mr. Miller. Come in."

Mr. Miller, uneasy with the cameras following his movements, stepped into the room, followed closely by Beth Connors, his daughter's best friend. Tony and Sully exchanged glances. Beth Connors blushed. Mr. Miller said to Tony, "They told me at the station that you'd be here. I just wanted to thank you again, detective. I appreciate all the hard work you've done for me and Nancy. I also wanted to tell you that I'm taking your advice."

"My advice?"

"Well, you gave me the idea. Beth and I," he inclined his head towards the blushing girl "are leaving for Scotland. We're joining my salmon fishing relatives."

Tony said, "That's great!"

"And that's not all. Beth and I are to be wed. We decided to stop by on the way to the airport."

"Hey!" Tony wrung Mr. Millers hand and said, "That's great! Congratulations!"

Beth blushed, smiled and showed off her ring to Deirdre and Courtney.

Sully thumped Mr. Miller on the back and said, "Good for you. Wish you the best."

When Mr. Miller, his bride to be, the reporters and Sully had left, the room felt unusually quiet. Tony took Deirdre by the hand and said, "Sorry you don't have a ring yet."

Deirdre waved his apology aside and said, "Pfft. I'll ask the nurse for a bandage to wrap around my finger." She kissed him. "It's you I want."

"It won't come to that. Believe me." Tony stepped back, took both of Deirdre's hands and said, "I was wondering… I thought it might be nice to wheel you around Venice for a week or two."

"Venice Beach?... in Florida?" Deirdre thought, *"Oh no. That's where my dad lives!"*

"Nope. Not Venice as in Florida. Venice as in gondolas, Italian music, romantic views... It would be a heck of a honeymoon."

Deirdre's jaw dropped. "Italy! No way!"

"Way."

"But how can we afford it? I don't have much money..."

"You know that talk-show host I can't stand? Donna Wells from the Good Morning with Donna Show? She's payin' for it. We might have a camera crew following us around for a day. If that's OK with you, I mean."

"Yeah. I think that's more than OK."

Be sure to read book 2 of the Detective Capella crime novel series:

DAUGHTER OF THE DON

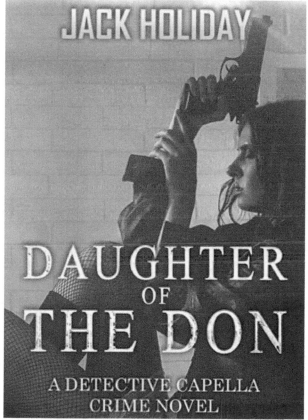

While investigating the Nancy Miller case, Boston Detective Tony Capella had fallen for the petite blonde now sleeping beside him. He wasn't sure if he believed in love at first sight, even so, their transcontinental flight was speeding them towards their wedding. What Tony didn't know was that the troubles they thought they'd left behind, in America, were not.

Join Tony, Deirdre and Courtney in a tale of kidnapping, murder, love and betrayal. A journey that leads them from Venice to Southern Italy, where lying in wait is the beautiful and utterly ruthless, Adelina Vittorio, the *Daughter of the Don*.

Please enjoy the first three chapters of *Daughter of the Don*:

Chapter 1
The Job

Two men, bound and gagged, lay on the Turkish rug. One of the men grimaced in pain as the black hose running beneath his thigh heated. The hose snaked across the living room floor in one direction, out the broken window of the Italian villa, and disappeared into the back of a white milk truck. The other end of the hose wound its way up the marble stairs, down a hall, into a lavish bedroom, coming to an end in a walk-in closet by a young man kneeling beside a massive steel safe.

The veins on the backs of his hands stood out as he held the drill in position. The muscles in his arms and chest were cast in vivid relief by the light from the bedroom. Dull titanium drill bits littered the floor. Twenty seven years old and ruggedly handsome, Rico paused, wiped the sweat from his brow with his forearm and looked over his shoulder. Standing in the doorway, blocking his light, was his younger sister.

Adelina's silhouette stood outlined in the doorway, dressed all in black: sports bra, spandex pants, ankle length boots and a nylon tactical belt slung low on her hip, bearing a silenced pistol and an assortment of razor-sharp throwing knives.

"Adelina, what are you doing? You're supposed to be in the truck with the equipment."

Brow furrowed, chin thrust forward in defiance, Adelina said, "How come I'm supposed to be in the truck? How come you're not in the truck?"

Rico, exasperated, said, "Now is not the time, Adelina. Get back in the truck. I'm almost done here. Go get things ready."

Adelina looked down at her older brother with a scowl and started to open her mouth. Seeing the look in her brother's eyes, Adelina bit back her retort and with a grunt, turned on her heel and left the room. Rico picked up the heavy drill, squirted some oil on the bit, and went back to work.

Thin corkscrews of shiny steel fell from the bit, making a glittering pile on the floor. As the drill bit passed through the inside wall of the safe, Rico took a deep breath and pulled it out. He held the bit to the light coming from the bedroom and was pleased to see the end covered with a thin film of gold. Rico picked up the thick black hose and slid the shiny tungsten end into the hole he had just drilled. From a toolbox he pulled a steel strap, placed it over the hose and screwed it securely to the floor with a battery operated drill. Rico clicked the talk button on his walkie-talkie and said, "Start the gas."

From the small speaker, Adelina's voice said, "Done."

Rico pressed a red button several times creating a spark with the pezio-electric crystal inside the safe. On the third press he could hear the torch kick to life with the roar of a blast furnace. Rico again used his walkie-talkie to call down to Adelina, "Up the gas and turn up the power on the heating coil."

Again he heard Adelina's monosyllabic reply, "Done."

Rico thought, *"This had better work..."* It had all been his idea. He had explained it to his father weeks ago...

"Papa," he had said, "One hole! One hole is all we need!"

His father had sat back in his leather armchair and shaken his head. "How, Rico? How are you going to get one thousand kilos of gold out of a safe with one hole? It's impossible."

"Heat, Papa. We take a hose and inside that hose we run four smaller hoses: two of them for oxygen and acetylene to melt the gold, one for a vacuum line to suck the molten gold out and another to suck out the exhaust fumes. We'll have to heat the hose as well to keep the gold from turning solid as we pump it..."

Rico's father sat in thought and reached for a cigar case that was no longer there. Disappointed, he withdrew his hand and said, "Hmm... That safe is state of the art. It's supposed to be uncrackable... If this could work..."

Rico pulled a paper from his pocket and passed it to his father. "See, the melting point of gold is about 1000° Celsius. Oxy acetylene gas will give us 3500°, thermite burns at 5000° but in an enclosed space such as a safe we won't need it. At 3500° we shouldn't even need to heat the hose, but just in case, we can wrap it with an electric heating coil."

Rico's father asked, "How long before you can try it?"

"A month, maybe less. We can do trials with lead, do surveillance on the Gambaro's villa and we'll have to re-enforce the suspension of a truck..."

Rico's father thought, *"Stealing gold from the Gambaro family will bankrupt them."* He nodded his consent and said, "Don Gambaro is a romantic fool to store all his money in gold. Get started." As Rico turned to leave, his father had said, "I want Adelina to work with you."

Rico didn't argue. Nobody argued with Rico's father and lived to tell about it.

Rico aimed a laser thermometer at the safe and read it's

outside temperature. *"1200° C, any hotter and the steel's going to melt... Then again it has to be nearly empty,"* he thought.   Sure enough, moments later, Rico heard the satisfying sound of the vacuum sucking air.

As Rico walked down the stairs he could smell something burning... burning flesh. As he came into the living room, he could see the two men he had left bound and gagged lying still. He walked over to their lifeless bodies and saw a bullet hole in each of their foreheads. The man with the heated hose running under one of his legs was giving off plumes of black acrid smoke. Rico gagged and swore under his breath. He crossed the room quickly, stepped up onto the windowsill and hopped lightly down to the ground. As he took a breath of fresh air, he looked around to see that no one had been alerted to his presence.

Rico opened one of the back doors of the truck. The escaping heat hit him in the face like an oven. Adelina stood in a silver heat suit, the kind worn by volcanologists when working on active volcanoes. A stream of gold flowed from the end of the hose, which she held with an asbestos mitt. Adelina moved the end of the hose over the molds as a baker making cupcakes. When the last drops of molten gold dripped into the last of the empty ingot molds, Adelina turned off the flow of oxygen and acetylene and switched off the power to the heater coil. Rico put one arm over his face and reached in for a pair of heavy cutters. Grasping the long handles, he took the cutter to the black hose and like a proud father, cut the umbilical of his "brain child". Rico jumped into the driver's seat, started the truck and put it in first gear. With over a ton of gold weighing down the truck, the engine protested, then quieted down as he picked up speed. With the windows open, the truck lost the feel of Dante's inferno. Rico spoke into his walkie talkie, "Everybody move out." Men slipped from the doors of the villa and from behind trees; non-descript men, dressed as field workers, who disappeared into the surrounding woods.

Adelina finished stripping off her heat suit, slid into the cab and dropped into the passenger seat. 22 years old, she moved with the grace of a panther. Her jet-black hair and piercing eyes, light brown, almost golden eyes, had always reminded Rico of a panther as well.

Cradled in an asbestos mitt, Adelina held one of the gold ingots, which sparkled in the sun. Gazing at the ingot she asked, "Can I have this one?"

Rico, not taking his eyes from the road said, "Sure. Why not?" Adelina laughed with pleasure. Rico took a quick glance at the ingot and asked, "What's so special about that one?"

"The gold in this one was coming out a little chunky. I was afraid that the hose was going to get clogged. As the ingot filled I could see little specs of green, red and clear sinking to the bottom and realized that they were emeralds, rubies and diamonds. There must have been some jewelry in the safe as well as the gold."

Those gems could be worth a fortune, but Rico had already said yes...

As they turned onto the main road, Rico remembered the two dead men. His orders had been clear: No killing if it could be avoided. They were out to bankrupt the Gambaros, not kill them... Rico didn't like to be made the fool, even by his little sister. He asked, "Was it necessary to kill those two men? You knew who they were."

Adelina kicked off her boots, lay back in her seat and hung her bare feet out the window. She put her hands behind her head and said, "You're too soft, Rico. You've always been too soft, even when we were children. Remember that fox we found in the trap? The one that you wanted to let go?"

Rico remembered. It still made him uncomfortable to think back on that day. He could picture the scene in his mind… Adelina in her pretty dress, bashing the fox's head in with a stone. She had been covered in gore and laughing her head off. When he had turned away she had called him a baby. Rico said, "It's one thing to bankrupt a rival family, it's another to kill their men. Do we really want a war?"

Adelina smiled and said, "I do. I'll show father who his worthy successor is. I don't think he'll choose a weakling like you."

Rico glanced in the rearview mirror and asked, "You think he'll choose a hot-head like you Adelina? You just killed Don Gambaro's sons. If you were Don, you'd have the whole of Sicily on fire within a week."

Adelina drew her feet in from the window, leaned forward towards Rico and said, "And our family would rise from the ashes like a phoenix and be the one great family that Sicily hasn't seen in a thousand years."

Chapter 2
Transatlantic

A fourteen hour flight. Tony stretched his legs. He was bored out of his mind. He'd have liked to look out the window, but he'd done the "gentlemanly" thing and had given Deirdre the window-seat. Deirdre was curled up next to him, fast asleep and looking beautiful. It was hard to imagine that just a few months earlier she had been a bloody mess. The scenes of her ordeal flashed in Tony's mind's eye, from her hit and run "accident", to her close brush with death. How Tony had been given the case to investigate the death of Miss Nancy Miller, who had been murdered for her pristine organs, transplanted into a rich Dubai businessman, and her AB negative blood, which only 1% of the world populace has. Tony had followed several false leads, but had solved the case just as the head surgeon and his nurse were preparing the same fate for Deirdre and her organs. Tony's partner, Sully, had shot the surgeon, Dr. Pritchett, to death and Pritchett's nurse was sitting in a cell awaiting trial. Tony and Deirdre still hadn't discussed it in detail and Tony didn't want to push it. He figured it best to give her some time and to be there when she was ready to talk about it. While investigating the Nancy Miller case, he had fallen for the petite blonde now sleeping beside him. Tony wasn't sure if he believed in love at first sight, even so, their transatlantic flight was speeding them towards their wedding.

Tony had become somewhat of a celebrity just before his promotion to Detective on the Boston Police Department. He had stopped several terrorists from pumping a van full of mustard gas into the MBTA subway system's ventilation system. A few weeks later, he had uncovered the murders in the Boston Trauma Center. According to the press, this elevated Tony from celebrity to star. Tony looked over his shoulder at an attractive blond with mile long legs, big hair and a big personality to match, Donna Wells, host of the talk show "Good Morning with Donna". Tony had been approached by all sorts of news media, but "Good Morning with Donna" had offered to fly Tony, Deirdre and Deirdre's best friend and Maid of Honor, Courtney, to Venice and to pay for everything: airfare, hotel and the wedding itself. It had seemed like a great idea at the time. The thought of just getting away…

A steady line of passengers, stewardesses and even the pilot, had stopped to chat with Donna and ask for her autograph. Twelve hours into the flight and her smile hadn't faltered. Tony wondered if Botox injections had frozen her smile in place. Donna caught Tony's eye, excused herself from the passengers she was speaking with and walked over. A man sitting to Tony's right in the aisle seat was a member of the "Good Morning with Donna" crew. Donna looked down at the man and raised one eyebrow. The realization that Donna wanted to sit down came slowly to the man, yet when it did, he sprang up like a jack in the box and disappeared down the aisle.

Donna took his empty seat and asked, "Tony, Tony, Tony, are you excited?"

Tony stifled a yawn and said, "Right now I'm more cramped than excited. I can't wait to move around. How can you stand it?"

Donna's smile widened. She leaned in conspiratorially and said, "Honey, try living on 1200 calories a day. After that, a fourteen hour flight is nothing." Donna inclined her head towards Deirdre and said, "Do you think you can wake up sleeping beauty? We'll be landing in Paris soon and I need to go over a few things with both of you."

Even though Donna was drop dead gorgeous, Tony thought her bossiness and take charge attitude made her somewhat mannish. He nodded and said, "I'll see what I can do." As he sat looking steadily at Donna, she realized that she was dismissed and that Tony intended to wake Deirdre up in his own way and alone. Donna got up and went back to her seat.

Tony might not like Donna very much, but he did respect her for being a hard worker and a professional. He looked down at Deirdre and thought that "sleeping beauty" wasn't too far from the mark. He got halfway out of his seat and gave Deirdre a light kiss on the lips. As Deirdre woke, she returned the kiss and opened her eyes. "Hey," she whispered.

Tony smiled, "Hey, back at ya." Deirdre's sparkling eyes spoke volumes. Tony thought, *"Damn you're beautiful"* and said, "Damn, you're beautiful."

A voice from the seat in front of Tony said, "Beautiful? Women want to be called "hot", Tony, not beautiful. Let's try it again. Damn, you're hot! You are so smokin' hot Dee." Courtney's head popped up from behind the seat. Instead of neon blue or bubblegum pink, Courtney had dyed her hair blonde for the wedding. Courtney looked from Tony to Deirdre. "Come on, Tony," she said, "You are so smokin' hot, Dee. Try it."

Deirdre reached over and pinched Courtney's lips closed with her thumb and forefinger. Deirdre glowered at her and said, "You are such a buzz kill, Courtney. You know that?"

Deirdre furrowed her brows and scowled as she shook her fist with her free hand. As Deirdre let go of Courtney's lips they both laughed.

Tony rolled his eyes and said, "Gee, Court, way to ruin the moment."

Courtney patted Tony on the cheek and said, "Come on, Tony. You know I love you guys."

Tony did know it. After Deirdre's brush with death, Courtney had been there for her. She'd been there after the operation on Deirdre's leg and she'd been there in a way that Tony couldn't hope to be. Sometimes a girl needs a girlfriend and Courtney was the best. Tony took Courtney's hand and said, "Love you, too, Court."

Courtney's eyes shot open. She looked to Deirdre and asked, "What's gotten into him? Must be altitude sickness."

Tony nodded and said, "Must be, yeah. That's gotta be it."

"You're not sick, are you, Tony?" Donna Wells had walked up unnoticed to the group. She looked at Tony with concern.

Tony thought for a moment how easy it would be to say, *"Yeah, I'm feeling pretty sick. I don't think I'll be able to do all the photo stuff, just the wedding."* That made him smile. He said, "No, no, I'm fine. What's up?"

Donna took the seat next to Tony and said, "We'll be landing in Paris in about an hour and I thought I'd fill you in on what to expect and what's expected of you."

The quad Rolls-Royce Trent 900 engines whined in reverse thrust as the Airbus A380 came in for a landing. Deirdre held the arms of her seat tightly, expecting a jolt as the tires hit the tarmac. She was surprised when all she felt was a slight thump. It wasn't long until their plane was docked at the terminal and passengers were scrambling for their carry on bags. As Deirdre started to stand, Tony put his hand lightly on her shoulder and shook his head. Deirdre sat and realized that those rushing to get off the plane would be standing for a while.

Their little group, consisting of Deirdre, Tony, Courtney, Donna Wells and her crew, assembled just inside the terminal. When they were all together, Donna Wells said, "Okay, people, customs first and then on to our first photo op."

Tony asked, "What about our luggage?"

Donna rolled her eyes and said, as if to a child, "All our luggage will be waiting at the hotel, Tony."

The group followed Donna like chicks following a

mother hen, all except for Courtney, who kept stopping to point out interesting things and people in the airport.

When they reached customs, Deirdre saw a long white counter, behind which stood uniformed customs officials who were rifling through the passenger's carry-on bags. When it was Donna Wells' turn, the customs official smiled, asked for her autograph and gave her bag a cursory inspection. Tony was next and the official going through his bag was far more thorough. His belongings were spread over the counter. When they were finished, Tony scooped his possessions back into his bag, pressed them down and zipped it up. Deirdre, remembering what she had in her bag, turned pale. As she walked up to the counter she held her bag tightly to her chest.

"Open your bag, please," said the customs official.

Deirdre leaned towards him and in hushed voice said, "Can we do this somewhere... somewhere more private?"

The customs official's brows came together. He said, "That would be somewhat irregular, Miss. Please open your bag."

Deirdre's face went from milky white to scarlet as she held the bag all the more tightly to her chest. The customs official, thoroughly suspicious now, started to signal some of his comrades. Tony took in the situation at once and said to the official, "Hold on just a sec. Look, I'm a cop, you're a cop. I'm sure this is some kind of woman thing; something that you and I probably wouldn't get." The official wasn't impressed. Tony hurriedly added, "We're here with the "Good Morning with Donna" show. Isn't there something you can do?"

The words "Good Morning with Donna" seemed to act like magic.

The customs official said, "Of course, of course. He signaled to a young woman inspector and told her to bring Deirdre into one of the inspection rooms.

When Deirdre heard the door click shut behind her she let out a sigh of relief. She put her carry-on bag down on the small white table in the middle of the room and unzipped it. The female customs inspector was about the same age as Deirdre. The moment she reached into Deirdre's bag she understood why Deirdre didn't want to open it in a public setting. One after another the inspector pulled pieces of lingerie from the bag. As she held up a black lace and mesh teddy, her brows went up and she smiled. She said, "Ooh la la. Très chic."

Deirdre returned her smile, blushed and thought, *"Wow. French people actually say Ooh la la."* Deirdre said, "They're for my honeymoon. I didn't want to take the chance of my luggage being lost... I mean..."

The Inspector came around the table, gave Deirdre a hug and said, "No, no, no. This is fine. Congratulations. Your fiancé, it is the young man with the dark hair, no?"

Deirdre nodded and said, "Yes."

The Inspector zipped Deirdre's bag closed and said, "He is very handsome. I wish you much joy." The Inspector held up her hand and moved her wedding ring about with her thumb. "I was recently married myself."

Deirdre said, "Oh, congratulations! How was your wedding?"

The french Inspector closed her eyes and smiled as if in ecstasy. "It was très fantastique!"

Deirdre put her hands on her hips and said, "Really?"

The Inspector opened her eyes and said, "Oh, yes. We have a tradition in France. Before a woman is wed, she sits down with the married women of her family and they share their secrets of pleasing their man on the wedding night. These secrets are passed down from generation to generation."

Deirdre's mouth dropped open and she said, "Wow. That's some tradition."

The Inspector sat on the corner of the table and said, "Yes, it is. That way the secrets are never lost, the men are happy and never stray. Would you like to hear some of the secrets?"

Deirdre pulled the fiberglass chair from beneath the table, spun it about and sat with her arms crossed on the back of the chair. She said, "Yes. I would definitely like that."

45 minutes later the inspector escorted Deirdre back to the waiting group, who had all finished with customs. Deirdre thought, *"This is going to be a wonderful trip."*

While Deirdre was having her tête-à-tête with the inspector, Donna Wells ushered the rest of the group out of customs and into the main airport. Waiting for them, just outside the doors were television and tabloid reporters, as well as the paparazzi. Tony found himself under a battery of flashing camera lights, which he found quite disconcerting. Courtney, on the other hand smiled and sprang into action. Playing on Tony's discomfiture, she stepped next to him and dropped into a pinup girl pose from the days reminiscent of World War II bomber plane nose art, having seen the poses in tattoo form on her many customers at the beauty salon. Courtney changed effortlessly from one pose to the next and seemed to be having the time of her life. As the photographers shot picture after picture, she put one arm around Tony and said, "Come on Tony, live a little. Have some fun."

Donna Wells shook her head and gritted her teeth. This was not going the way she had planned. She walked over and took both Tony and Courtney by the elbows and marched them back into the customs room. She turned on Courtney and exclaimed, "What was that all about?"

Courtney laughed and said, "Come on, Donna. You know they're going to eat that right up."

Donna stood, looking stern and cocked her head to one side, "You know, you're probably right? I didn't think of it from that angle."

A moment later Deirdre slipped her arm into Tony's and

gave him a winning smile. Tony asked, "What took you so long? They didn't give you a hard time, did they?"

Deirdre shook her head and said, "Oh, no. Not at all."

Tony looked closely at Deirdre and said, "Okay, well, I just want everything on our trip to be perfect."

Deirdre smiled and said, "I know it will, Tony."

Donna clapped her hands and said loudly, "Okay, people, we're off to the hotel." She beckoned to one of the customs officials and asked, "Is there another way out of here? I don't want to relive that last press op."

The customs official led the group through a door and down a long hallway. He spoke briefly to a uniformed guard at a double set of doors who opened them. The group walked out into the French sunshine and to the waiting limousines.

Chapter 3
The Family

The Vittorio family stood, sat and paced under the shade of a portico outside the family villa, waiting for the meeting to start. Tony, some of his cousins and several Caporegimes (or under-bosses) known as "Capa's", milled about or chatted. In a corner, standing alone, Capa Bartoli drained his glass of sambuca in one long pull and refilled it from a bottle on a side table. Rico held a glass of lemon water. He wondered why liquor was available at all. His father would throw a person out of a meeting for being the slightest bit liquored up. Rico took a date from a platter, knelt down and handed it to a squirrel that was sitting behind one of the columns. The squirrel took it in his tiny hands and scampered into the bushes. When Rico looked up, Capa Bartoli was standing over him, reeking of sambuca. Rico stood quickly. Capa Bartoli, an uneasy half smile on his face said, "Rico, how are you? It's good to see you. It's been a long time."

Rico looked displeased. He knew he should probably keep his mouth shut, but Bartoli had been part of the family ever since he could remember. He asked, "Capa, what's bothering you? You're drinking like a fish. You know my father hates that."

Capa Bartoli hung his head and looked at his shoes. He said, "Rico, that's just the thing, your father... he gave me a job and it didn't go so well. I was hoping that maybe you could put in a good word for me."

Rico took an involuntary step back from Bartoli. On Mount Olympus, one is just as easily struck by stray lightning. If Bartoli botched a job, no good word of Rico's would do him a bit of good and Bartoli had to know that. Rico shook his head and said, "Capa, you know there's only one thing you can do if you fail at a job. Do yourself a favor and stop drinking now. When you see my father, remember that you're a Capa and do the right thing."

Bartoli nodded and walked back to his bottle.

Rico could hear Adelina's laugh coming from a group of trees a short distance from the portico. He picked up his lemon water and walked towards the sound. As he came around the little grove, one of his cousins was handing Adelina a thick wad of money. Adelina asked, "Want to try again?"

The young man shook his head and said, "Maybe later. You've taken all my money."

Adelina laughed, slapped him on the back and said, "Let that be a lesson to you. Never gamble all of your money, even if it is against a woman."

Rico stood leaning against a tree and watched his sister as she pulled her knives, one by one, from the wooden target. Rico sighed and said, "Why do you take all the young men's money, Adelina? You throw knives better than a gypsy."

Adelina slipped the last knife into her belt. She said, "I should. I learned how to throw from the gypsies. The young men think that just because I am a woman, I'm no good. I like to prove them wrong and if it makes them hurt a little, all the better." Adelina pulled a knife and handed it, handle first, to her brother. She asked, "How about you, Rico? Do you still know how to throw?"

Rico took the knife on his palm and felt it's weight. While still looking Adelina in the eye, he swung his arm in a tight arc, releasing the knife by his thigh. When Adelina looked, the knife was sitting squarely in the center of the target.

"How do you do that, Rico? You didn't even look at the target. Show me."

Rico smiled and said, "Say: please." Rico had only heard Adelina say please once in her life and that was to their father.

Adelina was torn between wanting to learn something

new with the knife and having to say that dreaded word. Finally, through clenched teeth, she said, "Please."

Rico took one look at the target and turned his back on it. He looked at Adelina and said, "It's easy. All you have to do is believe that you can do it. Watch." Rico, again, threw the knife low by his thigh and, again, heard the sound of it striking the target.

Adelina looked dumbfounded. She said, "That's it? I have to believe?"

Rico pulled the knife from the target and handed it to her, "That's it. It's that simple. The first time I saw it done, I didn't believe it either. Now you do it."

Adelina looked at the target and turned her back on it. Rico knew she would miss before she even threw. He pulled another knife from her belt and put it in her hand. He said, "That's not the way, Adelina. You really have to believe that you can do it. I've seen you with a knife. If anyone can do it, you can, but you have to believe it. Be confident. Now throw."

Adelina started to throw and stopped herself. Rico watched as her eyes became fierce like the panther's. This time he knew she would hit before she threw. At the sound of the knife hitting the target, Adelina smiled. She didn't turn around; instead she pulled one knife after another and sank them into the wood.

As Adelina slid her knives back into her belt, one of the servants, who was also a cousin, came out to tell them that their father was ready to start the meeting. As they walked back to the house, Adelina gave Rico a rare smile. It was rare in that it had affection for her brother behind it.

When they entered the villa, they found most of their family seated. Rico walked over towards his father and sat at his right hand, Adelina to his left. Don Vittorio cleared his throat and the room went silent. He looked at the assembled faces and said, "Excuse me for not standing. For some time, I have not been well. First, I am, both, pleased and proud to announce that my son, Rico with the help of my daughter, Adelina, have, in one stroke, both bankrupted the Gambaro family and increased the Vittorio fortune by forty million American dollars."

The room erupted in applause, which was quieted by Don Vittorio motioning palm downwards with his hands. Don Vittorio continued, "As I say, I have not been well. I am, I know no other way to put this but simply, I am in need of a kidney... Which brings me to Capa Bartoli." Don Vittorio spoke softly and gently, but everyone in the room listened with their full attention, "Bartoli, would you please step up here."

Bartoli wiped the sweat from his forehead and got unsteadily to his feet. He walked as a man walks to the electric chair, with a shuffling, nervous gait. He stopped before Don Vittorio and clasped his hands. He glanced briefly at Rico and said, "Don Vittorio forgive me. You gave me a job and I failed you."

As Bartoli hung his head, Don Vittorio said, "Not only did you fail to get me a kidney, you paid a great deal of the family money, which, as I understand, you cannot get back. Is that correct?"

Capa Bartoli nodded and said, "Yes, Don Vittorio."

Don Vittorio sat and considered. Finally, when it seemed the silence could grow no thicker, Don Vittorio nodded and said, "I will forgive you."

Forgiveness to some means one thing. Forgiveness in the Vittorio family could mean many things: a pat on the back, or a quick death. Don Vittorio looked to his son and said, "Rico, would you –"

Adelina interrupted and said, "Papa, let me. I'm sorry to interrupt, Papa, but Rico taught me something new today and I would love to show you."

Don Vittorio considered his daughter and then looked to his son. The honor of carrying out Don Vittorio's orders went to Rico.

Rico looked back at his father, shrugged and said, "It's all right with me, Papa."

Don Vittorio looked at his daughter and nodded. Adelina stood, walked over and took Bartoli by the arm. Happily, as if they were playing a game at a birthday party, she said, "Come, I want you to stand right here." She led him across the room and positioned him with his back to the wall.

Adelina crossed to the other side of the room and drew two knives from her belt. She looked to her father for permission to proceed, which he gave with a nod. Adelina surprised everyone in the room except Rico, when she turned and faced away from Bartoli. Rico couldn't see her face, but could picture it clearly. He knew she had the look of the panther. With hardly any arc at all, Adelina's razor sharp knives shot from her hands and buried themselves deep in Bartoli's chest, pinning him to the wall. The room, once again, broke into applause. Adelina turned about and bowed this way and that, a self satisfied smile on her face.

Don Vittorio waited until Bartoli's foot stopped twitching and continued, "Now, about this kidney. I've personally arranged for it to be delivered to Italy. It should be arriving in Venice tomorrow. Rico, I need you to take some of our men and pick it up for me."

Rico stood, "I'll bring it back, Papa."

Daughter of the Don is the second in the Detective Capella series, following *Murder in the E.R.*

DAUGHTER OF THE DON

_____END_____

Jackie's latest novel, She Rises, is a moving portrait of young love, overcoming insurmountable odds and the strength of friendship.

She Rises

List of Characters

Nancy Miller	Victim number 1
Tony Capella	Detective
Captain Rodriguez	Police Capt.
Mustafa Califf	Organ recipient
Deirdre McDonough	Heroine
Detective Sullivan	Tony's partner
Dr. Pritchett	Head of Surgery
Nurse Harris	head emergency room nurse
Courtney	Deidre's roommate
Donald Miller	Nancy's father
Frank Green	Hospital CEO
Harold Ross	Big boss, Whitney and Brown
Daniel Whitcomb	Nancy's boss
Sean	Police I.T. dept, electronic forensics
Bill Matthews	Nancy's flirty co-worker
Beth Connors	Nancy's friend
Craig Morris	Mortician
Henrique Parreira	Fugitive
Sergeant Avilla	Fall River Police

About the Author

Jackie Holiday was born the fourth of six children. If given the opportunity to meet Jackie Holiday, if only for a moment, you would never forget it! There is nothing predictable about Jackie, or Jackie's stories. Jackie has a deep love for language, history, and the arts. Jackie Holiday holds a Bachelor of Science in electrical engineering and is an accomplished foil fencer. Jackie has a special talent of incorporating bits and pieces of an amazing life into the lives of Jackie's characters. When asked about accomplishments for this books' jacket, Holiday didn't care to enumerate a long list of academic awards, patents, and copyrights; instead, Jackie said, "I've always done my best to be good, and to be kind to people. That's what's most important when we're writing our own stories. It's much harder to be a hero than a villain. My motto is: Love others, and love yourself. I'm just happy knowing that I've tried hard to be good, and that I'll continue trying to do my best." Readers will agree that we see the best of Jackie Holiday with "Murder in the E.R."

Acknowledgments

I would like to express my gratitude to all the people who encouraged me in the writing of Murder in the E.R. Many, many thanks to my Mother, my sister Maia and my four brothers: Ted, David, Jonathan and Christopher for their generous inspiration. Thanks to Graeme and Ani for their martial arts prowess. Thank you, Claire. Sincere thanks go out to the Boston Police Department, the Fall River Police Department, and all our men and women in blue for their dedicated service to us all. Thank you, God. To each and every reader thank you! Thank you for your love of reading and for choosing to spend your time with the characters of Murder in the E. R.

Murder in the E. R.

Made in the USA
Middletown, DE
16 January 2023

22302267R00116